About the

Anna's adult life has been moulded a great deal by challenges to her physical health and the need to adapt to them. She was diagnosed with Neurofibromatosis type 2 (NF2) in the 1990s and went deaf soon after, while at university. She then began to learn British Sign Language to help with communication and loved it immediately, becoming fluent enough to teach it.

In the last seven years, Anna's vision has deteriorated and she is now registered deaf–blind. That and other health complications led her to stop working. Although sad to leave a job she loved, she is now relishing having more time to write and much of her writing is greatly influenced by her desire to share the realities of living with disability.

Anna wrote and self-published a semi-autobiographical novel called *Catch It Anytime You Can* in 2012 and also loves writing poetry, short stories and articles. *Senseless* is her first full-length work of fiction.

Apart from writing, Anna loves horse riding and competes at dressage with the RDA (Riding for the Disabled Association). She will be donating 10% of her royalties from *Senseless* to St Ives (Bingley) RDA where she has weekly lessons.

SENSELESS

SENSELESS

SENSELESS

ANNA LICKLEY

This edition first published in 2018

Unbound

6th Floor Mutual House, 70 Conduit Street, London W1S 2GF

www.unbound.com

ISBN (eBook): 978-1-912618-05-7

ISBN (Paperback): 978-1-912618-04-0

Design by Mecob

Printed in Great Britain by Clays Ltd, Elcograf S.p.A

Senseless is dedicated to the memory of Ken Lickley
Der beste Vater der Welt
1946 – 1999

Dear Reader,

The book you are holding came about in a rather different way to most others. It was funded directly by readers through a new website: Unbound.

Unbound is the creation of three writers. We started the company because we believed there had to be a better deal for both writers and readers. On the Unbound website, authors share the ideas for the books they want to write directly with readers. If enough of you support the book by pledging for it in advance, we produce a beautifully bound special subscribers' edition and distribute a regular edition and e-book wherever books are sold, in shops and online.

This new way of publishing is actually a very old idea (Samuel Johnson funded his dictionary this way). We're just using the internet to build each writer a network of patrons. Here, at the back of this book, you'll find the names of all the people who made it happen.

Publishing in this way means readers are no longer just passive consumers of the books they buy, and authors are free to write the books they really want. They get a much fairer return too – half the profits their books generate, rather than a tiny percentage of the cover price.

If you're not yet a subscriber, we hope that you'll want to join our publishing revolution and have your name listed in one of our books in the future. To get you started, here is a £5 discount on your first pledge. Just visit unbound.com, make your pledge and type BETH18 in the promo code box when you check out.

Thank you for your support,
unbound-signatures-for-letter

Dan, Justin and John
Founders, Unbound

Super Patrons

Sue Ainley
Shirley & Nick
Jane Armstrong
Kate Bairstow
The Baldwin Family
Trudy Bean
Sarah Bellwood
Penelope Beschizza
Mary Bolton
Teresa Brasier
Leigh-Anne Brown
Rachel Butterfield
Alison Capey
Mandy Clift
Sarah Clilverd
Joanna Coleman
Geraldine Collie
Norman Cook
Peter Crawshaw
Valerie Cushing
Clive & Anne Davis
Pat de Reyes
Lynn Delfosse
Cherry Dexter
Sue Duke
Ivan & Jackie Dunn
Julia Elliot
Carol Fellingham Webb
Tom & Liz Franks
Judy Green
Vivien Halliwell
Mary Halsey

Susan Hargadon
Sheila Harris
Shaunett Harris
Samantha Havis
Jill Henshaw
Stephen Hey
Jade & Kirsty Higgs
Michelle Higgs
Jilly Holland
Louise Holland
Julie Holmes
Kate Houghton
John Howard
Ron Howard – in memory of Julie Howard
Karen Humphreys
Huw Huw
Lizzy Jackson
Mo Jackson
Sarah Jackson
Jackie Jackson-Smith
Liz Jobey
Bonnie Kelly
Dan Kieran
Sally Kingsley
Jean Leake
Tracey Leake
Susan Lee
Jill Lickley
Margaret Longden
Liz Macartney
Rodney Marsh
Jean Mcbean
Suzanne Meinert
Jill Merritt
Val Middleton
John Mitchinson

Heather Mole
Janet Montefiore
Andrew & Janet Munro
Carlo Navato
Hilary Nelmes
Pam Noble
Lucy Oldroyd
Steph Osborn
Katie Peat
Justin Pollard
John Popham
Andrew Pye
Anna Pye
Julie Ralph
Jen Rhodes
Bruce Rhodes
Hazel Rolston
Paul Scales
Brian Scott
Laura Sheard
Rosemary Silverson
Sylvia Simmonds
Tanya Simpson
Anna Smith
Paula Squire
Claire Stent
Sue Stevens
David Storer
Lynne Swarbrick Hughes
Mary Tibbett
Barbara Todd
Jonathan Tomkinson
Hilary Trickey
Ann Vear
Percy Vear
Henry Waddington

John Walker
Joanne Ward
Lisa Ward
Debbie Watkins
Lesley Weatherson-Emm
Josephine Wesley
Stephen Whitehead
Andrew Wight
Helen Williams
Hazel Williams
Amy Wilson
Jube Wiseman
Kate Wood
Anya Woodbridge
Marjorie Woodhams
Sara Yarnell

With thanks to Andrew Pye who helped to make this book happen.

Chapter 1

'The Better Solutions honchos are a nasty, money-grabbing bunch of wankers, Beth,' Rick was saying as they pulled up outside her house. 'For God's sake, you are 32 years young. What the hell are you doing in this pissy job?'

Beth was too tired to answer after they had driven a 400-mile round trip in heavy traffic to attend the Better Solutions UK AGM. She shook her head and shrugged instead.

'All we do is drive across half the country to care homes trying to persuade underpaid staff to buy Better Solutions bath hoists and Better bloody Solutions state–of–the–art wheelchair ramps.'

Rick paused for breath but Beth knew he wasn't stopping. She wondered sleepily how many times he'd said this to her in the course of the journey.

'These people only come to our demonstrations to get the free mugs, pens, mouse mats, cakes and whatever the fuck else we have to sweeten them up with. We're the ones feeling like bloody idiots slugging this stuff around and breaking our sodding backs in the process.'

'I know, Rick, maybe one day I really will get round to moving on but…'

'But what, Beth? "But" is what I've been saying all my life. We both have dreams of doing something else. What's stopping you?'

'I don't know,' she shrugged, rubbing her hand over her eyes, 'I'm too tired, Rick, I'll have to go in.'

'Alright, Beth love, I'll see you tomorrow.'

Beth pulled herself out of his overheated car and it was so cold that by the time she'd walked the 15 steps to her front door, the metal door handle felt wet to her frozen fingers.

'Fuck, fuck, fuck,' she chanted as she fumbled with her key, seeing a frozen cloud coming from her mouth. The only light was a faint glow from the distant street lamp but even that was obscured by an overgrown bush. There were no lights on in the house, so Dan was already in bed. He would usually leave the porch light on if Beth still hadn't come home from a long working day. He'd sometimes leave a note on the door for her too: *Come to bed immediately!* or *Welcome home, sexy!*

Tonight there were neither of those things. She was worried about Dan, he'd been in a strange, uncommunicative mood for the last few weeks. His sullen moods were very unlike him. After asking a couple of times if he was okay and getting the brush off, she had decided to ignore it and wait for the real Dan to come back. It was probably just work stress; he had mentioned budget cuts.

All Beth wanted now was to get this bloody rigid bra off and curl up in bed next to a calm, sleeping Dan hoping he'd wake up in a better mood tomorrow.

When she got in, the dark house was freezing. Had Dan not had the heating on at all tonight? She went to the lounge and bent to turn on the glass-fronted faux-flame gas fire, holding out her hands to the flames. That's when she noticed the envelope on the mantelpiece with BETH written in large black letters on the front. Had Dan left a welcome note after all? He'd never used an envelope before. She lifted it down drowsily, tempted to just put it in her pocket to read in the morning. But something about the formality of the sealed envelope made her open it. When she pulled out the folded piece of A4 paper there was just one short line in Dan's best cursive. Bile rose in her throat as she read the words:

I have loved you so much Beth, I'm so sorry. D xx

All thoughts of sleep suddenly vanished. 'Oh my God, Dan,' she screamed out, 'Dan! Dan!'

She ran to the kitchen and switched on the light; there was nothing there but a discarded half-drunk mug of cold tea.

'DAN?!'

She bolted to the stairs, running up them two at a time, and threw open the door to the box room they used as an office. It was empty. With a pounding in her chest, she wheeled round and checked the bathroom. It was also empty, towels slung carelessly on the floor where she had left them this morning in her haste to dress. God! Finally she threw open the door to their bedroom. The bed was unmade but the room was empty. Thank God! All she felt was relief. No Dan hanging by his neck or convulsed on the bed or slumped in a cold bath of bloodied water. But then the relief became despair. If the house was empty, Dan was gone.

Chapter 2

Luckily there was one space left as Beth pulled into the small car park. As she parked, she looked up at the tatty college. A lone boy kicked a ball against the wall and the thudding monotony echoed the pounding in her head. She struggled from the car and headed to Student Services with minutes to spare. 'Alright, Beth?' Diane, the head of department, greeted her, 'Tom just emailed, he won't be in today so can you go and work with Becky in her beauty class? Gemma usually does that, but she's off today.'

'Right,' Beth managed, trying to process Diane's quick-fire instructions as she watched her bustling off down the corridor. This was what it was always like, 'do this, go there, don't have an opinion on anything, just follow instructions and nod'. She was weary all the time. Working as a Communication Support Worker was supposed to be her dream, a chance for her to do something she enjoyed. She was beginning to wonder if there was anything that she would truly enjoy doing. Was she just destined to be dissatisfied forever?

She couldn't say she was sad not to be sitting with Tom. He was one of those skulking kids who sat slumped in his seat, arms folded in a protective barrage around his chest. He wasn't interested, didn't even watch the signing half the time. On top of that, she had a problem with his name. It was a common enough name but every time she heard it, she felt her stomach lurch with a longing for the only Tom who existed for her, the brother she had adored so much. Her mind was filled with the halcyon days of their childhood, when life was so smooth and unsullied by... She couldn't let her thoughts run away with her. *Say stop when your thoughts start drifting back to what happened*, she heard her therapist telling her.

The beauty school was on the ground floor of the college. They had a full corridor, with a hairdressing salon, a treatment room for practical sessions and four classrooms for teaching. Becky was in the treatment room this morning and the students who'd arrived were sitting paired up around the beds lining each side of the long room, making it look like a hospital ward. The bed covers were a washed-to-grey, greenish colour and Beth always felt slightly sick in here. Becky was sitting by the bed at the end of the row, fixing her hair in a low ponytail and looking around waiting for her CSW.

Morning, Beth signed, *Gemma's ill so it's me today.*

Cool. She smiled distractedly.

What's the plan today, do you know? I haven't seen the lesson plan.

I think we're doing waxing. We had a bit of a practice last week on our own legs but only quickly at the end. Today might be bikini lines.

Becky got her phone from her bag and started texting someone. Beth looked around to see that the class was pretty much all there and in pairs for working, chatting away to each other. Becky was still without a partner, immersed in her own world.

The teacher, Gail, walked in – a warm, plumpish woman in her fifties. The students glanced up at her and quieted down. Becky was still looking down at her phone, so Beth waved again to let her know that Gail had arrived.

'Are you all paired up?' Gail was asking, by the time Beth looked her way.

There were murmurs of 'yeah' from round the room. When Beth signed the question to Becky, her hand shot up.

'Becky doesn't have a partner,' Beth voiced.

'Oh, that's alright,' Gail replied, 'Gemma usually pairs up with Becky if she's on her own.'

Beth seethed internally. Bloody 'do-gooder' Gemma would, of course; but it wasn't right or fair to ask, surely?

'O-kay,' she forced out. Now wasn't the time to protest. Beth found this one of the hardest things about the job. She was here to aid Becky's communication, full stop. Her job description was pretty clear on that, but time and again she'd be asked to do extra things and was never sure what to do for the best.

She'd talked to Gemma about it once but her policy was to 'just do it', especially in the beauty classes when you'd get a free manicure or facial thrown in. Beth felt this wasn't helpful: how could you sign for Becky properly with a face pack on your face or fingers sticky with nail polish? She felt she was being taken for granted. At the same time, would it be churlish to refuse?

Gail was explaining the process of bikini waxing. 'You'll need hard wax, not the sort that requires muslin strips. It's better if you begin by using warm water and gently trimming stray hairs around the area...'

Beth realised that, this time, there was no way in hell that she was going to give in. She would *not* let a student wax her privates.

For now, she had to keep signing for Becky. Gail was explaining the different preferences of waxing: a neat triangle, a love heart, a full Brazilian. Becky looked slightly uncomfortable as Gail sent the class to the store room to get waxing kits and towels.

She seized this moment to grab Gail.

'Sorry, Gail, but I'm not comfortable with this. I don't mind the odd manicure and I'd be okay with a leg wax but bikini? No.'

'Becky is on her own then?'

'I'm here as Becky's CSW. I couldn't seriously do this support with someone who has waxed my privates.' The volume level of her voice was rising slightly and she swallowed, not wanting other students to overhear.

'Beth, I understand, love, but Becky needs a partner and I thought you were here to support her?'

'No... yes, but only for communication.' Beth was fuming internally but stuck for words. Tailing off, there was a silence so she tried again. 'I'm not sure the CSW should be doing any of the other stuff either but it's a tricky situation.' She fought to keep her voice calm.

'Yes, okay Beth, Becky can work in a three today.' A slightly harder edge had crept into Gail's voice, as if Beth was being unreasonable and they'd *talk about this later*.

At break time, Beth went to the canteen and got a coffee out of the machine. She'd picked a table in the corner where she could get a few minutes' quiet to herself. There was clattering from the kitchens where the catering students were preparing lunch. In just over an hour's time, there'd be huge metal trays of overcooked pasta shells in tomato gloop, and jacket potatoes and grated cheese served with a bit of iceberg lettuce and some sliced, tasteless tomato.

Gail came in and Beth fished her phone from her bag in order to look busy. Despite this, Gail brought her coffee over to the table. Beth sighed inwardly.

'You alright, Beth?'

That hadn't been what Beth was expecting. 'Yeah, all the better for a coffee.' She tried to smile.

'I know what you mean, what would we do without caffeine?' Gail smiled too, but she had a concerned look on her face. Beth wasn't sure if this was better or worse than a misinformed lecture about supporting the deaf students.

Silence fell. Gail broke it, saying conversationally, 'After lunch, we're watching a video about waxing and hygiene so can you sign that for Becky?'

'Is it subtitled?'

'No, you'll need to sign it.'

'Does it have a transcript?'

'No, it's old. It lasts about twenty-five minutes.'

'Twenty-five?!'

'Yes.'

'It would be a lot better if I had known and been able to watch it beforehand.' Beth's voice was strained. She signed to level 3; a fully qualified interpreter would have level 6 and would still want to familiarise themselves with the video before signing it to anyone. 'Becky is going to miss out on some of it. Not only because I haven't had any preparation to make sure Becky and I understand jargon signs, but because it is very difficult for a deaf person to watch a TV screen and an interpreter at the same time. You can't have eyes looking in two places at once.'

Beth was so tired of this. How many times did she have to remind them? Signing British Sign Language was not just gesturing and repeating what you heard. It was translating from English to another language.

'If you don't want to do it, Becky will miss out completely.'

Oh fuck off Gail, Beth thought, 'Yes, I KNOW that, but she will miss out anyway.'

'Well, Gemma doesn't usually mind doing it.'

It was all Beth could do not to explode with frustration. Bloody Gemma just signing whatever they asked only added to the problem, making the tutors think it was okay to work like this. Gemma had once told her, in her bloody little sing-song voice, that it was okay to miss some information, that some signing was better than no signing at all. She made it sound as if deaf students didn't have any rights to fair and equal learning.

'Excuse me, Gail.' Beth couldn't handle this any more, and pushed back her chair too quickly, knocking the table so that Gail's coffee sloshed over the sides of her cup. 'I just need to get something from my car.'

Half-running outside, she took a few gulps of air, fishing for the painkillers in her bag. She was so bloody angry, and she still, somehow, had to get through the rest of the day. She hated this fury that kept rising in her, and tried to take deep, slow, calming breaths like her therapist had taught her. If she could only get through today then at least she had this evening to look forward to.

Chapter 3

'You're wearing my walking socks!' Beth punched her brother.

'I am not, they'd be far too tiny. Mine are the same colour is all.'

'Where are mine then?'

'I don't know, Miss Bethany, but I will find them for you.'

Tom started scouting round the house, and she knew he would find them because it seemed he could do everything he set his mind to.

In a couple of days' time, he would be going away to university and she felt so sad. The house would feel empty without him.

They'd always gone on a good family ramble on Sunday mornings before coming home in plenty of time for Dad to make a Sunday roast while Mum put her feet up. Today would be no different.

Her dad walked in with his compass and a map in a clear wallet hanging round his neck: he loved the nerdy planning. Beth was more like her mum, and would just get out of a car and head down a track to see where it went, but Dad always had to have an intricate plan.

'Are you ready, treasure?' he asked, giving her a hug.

'As soon as Tom finds my socks.'

'What are you going to do without him? Walk in bare feet? Honest to God, that boy has been your protector from the moment you were born. He used to give you all his toys and toddle about watching Mum change your nappies.'

Just to emphasise his indispensability, Tom came back and waved a pair of socks over Beth's face, pulling them away just as she reached for them.

'Say thank you, ma'am!'

When they'd all climbed out of the car and squeezed through the stile, Mum and Dad walked ahead at a vigorous pace and Beth and Tom followed in their wake, huddled close against the wind.

11

'This might be our last ever family walk,' Beth lamented.

'No way, uni holidays are long, you know, and I'm not missing out on all the fun.' He pulled his coat around himself and hobbled crookedly.

Beth laughed, 'It IS fun though.'

'Yeah it is,' he said, throwing an arm round her shoulders. They paused to take it in. All they could see were fields and hills being grazed by ragged-looking sheep.

'Dad said you used to help Mum change my nappies,' Beth added.

'Of course I did, anything for you, Princess Girl.' He saw Beth's face, and added, 'Don't worry, I can't remember any of it so your dignity is intact. Hey anyway, are you ready for Tuesday?'

'What's happening on Tuesday?' Beth asked innocently.

Tom looked at her with a smile. 'You are winning a piano competition, Mozart.'

'Ah yes, that, I had forgotten.'

Tom gave her a playful thump, 'Yeah right! She who has been practising every hour of the day for the last month.'

'Lucky you will be here for it.'

'Wouldn't miss it for anything. Mind you, I don't *need* to be here for it, I have heard you play the tune eight hundred and seventy-two times already.'

'Which did you like best?'

'I thought the six hundredth and third time was the most resonant.'

'Right, I'll replicate that.'

Mum and Dad had stopped to let them catch up.

'What are you two plotting so earnestly?' Mum shouted over the wind.

'Only talking about Beth's moment of stardom on Tuesday.'

'What's happening on Tuesday?' said Mum. Tom and Beth cracked up in unison.

'God, you are two peas in a pod,' Tom wheezed, pulling Beth and his mum into a bear hug.

'What?'

'Beth made exactly the same wisecrack.'

'What *is* happening on Tuesday though?' Dad piped in.

'Da-ad!'

'I should know, Mum reminds me every day. We have a plan too, you know?'

'What kind of plan?'

'Well, not only are you being Mozart but I believe this little man here,' he gestured to Tom, who pulled a cutesy face, 'is off somewhere on Wednesday.'

'But we won't miss him,' Mum quipped.

'Of course we won't miss him,' Beth said, taking his arm. 'What are you planning?'

'Something good but if I tell you, I'd have to kill you.'

'Pfft, lead on then – or is it time for our Mars Bars yet?'

'No, it is not time for our energy-restoring Mars Bars – we've walked across two fields!'

Beth sighed and shook her head although she felt very happy, aware of having the best family ever.

Chapter 4

Sam Owens was sitting at his kitchen table, trying to talk to Kim while feeding Ollie. Unfortunately, Ollie had other ideas and seemed intent on making as much noise as possible by banging his flat hands on the table of his high chair.

'Oh, stop it, Ollie!' Kim turned to face her son, 'Just shut up for once and eat your food!'

She bent to lift his hands away from the table and Ollie seized the opportunity to grab a strand of her long dark hair. Sam knew that Kim had just spent at least half an hour washing, straightening and styling it.

'Ollie, get off! Sam, can't you control him for one second?'

'What?!' Sam tried not to shout; he was fed up with Kim's seeming inability to understand that a baby is a baby. Babies puke, shit and wail in equal measures.

Of course, Ollie started to wail now as Kim prised his hands from her hair and ran to the tap to wash out the baby food mush he'd left there.

Sam lifted Ollie from his seat and sat him on his lap, bouncing him up and down and letting him play with the straps of his hoodie.

When Ollie grew quieter, Sam gave him a rattle from the table to play with. He took advantage of the lull and said:

'I'm getting the results of my tests today. The GP wants me to go in and see him.'

'What tests?'

'The ones I told you about.'

She looked at him blankly.

'Kim! The tests I had after I'd seen the doctor about the tingly feelings in my hands and feet.'

'Oh that!' she said dismissively, 'Couldn't he just give you some pills?'

15

'He said he could but he wanted to give me some tests first. We talked about this, Kim!'

She didn't seem to register or react, still focused on combing out her hair with her fingers.

'I'm getting really tired and it's affecting my job,' Sam pushed.

'We all get tired!'

'Yeah well, you have to be completely on top of your game to fight fires.'

'I bet it's because Ollie is keeping you awake.'

'It's more than that, it's like I'm not functioning properly.'

'Right.'

'Are you even listening, Kim?'

'Of course I am,' she said, rooting in her handbag for her lipstick. 'You go to the GP and get some pills and you'll be right as rain. Don't forget to pick up my dress from the dry-cleaners, will you? I've got Pilates after I drop Ollie with his childminder.'

'Kim! There's more to life than picking up dresses from dry-cleaners.'

'Of course there is, but why do you need to become so dull?'

'Dull?! Are we even speaking the same language?'

'Ever since Ollie, you've been getting so dull, Sam. We never go out.'

'It's called being a parent! One day we all have to grow up.'

Kim scoffed and picked up Ollie. Sam went silent and just looked at her in disbelief. Everything had been so different before Ollie came along. She was 22 and gorgeous when they got together and as a tall, strong, 28-year-old firefighter, he had been exactly the action-hero sidekick she'd wanted. If they made it out of bed, he'd notice how many people turned to look at them anywhere they went together.

But now? Well, he didn't know what was happening now.

He was left to wait thirty-five minutes before Dr Longford was ready to see him. It gave him time to wonder if he should be more worried than he was. In truth, he couldn't get Kim, and the state of their relationship, out of his head.

When his name was called, he had a sudden panic; was there a reason he'd been called in or was it just routine?

He went along the corridor to clinic room number eight to find Dr Longford standing in the doorway to welcome him, his face giving nothing away.

'Ah, Sam, hello. Sit down, sit down.'

Sam waited while the doctor got his notes up on his computer and turned back to face him.

'Look, sorry, Sam, but I'm going to have to rush. I'm also sorry I kept you waiting. There's a meeting I need to get to by twelve so currently I have six minutes per patient if I'm going to make it.'

Sam shifted in his seat, wishing this to be over already. He felt unbalanced by the doctor's flustered spiel.

'Okay, so, as you know, the results of your tests have come back.' Dr Longford was starting to look uneasy and turned back to his computer screen, reluctant to meet Sam's eye. Sam braced himself for the revelation that he was dying of cancer, with months left to live.

'Go on,' he forced out when the pause became too long.

'Have you heard of multiple sclerosis, Sam?

'Yes.'

'Right, well, I'm sorry, but the tests show that you have it.'

'I have multiple sclerosis?'

'Yes.'

Sam laughed a nervous adrenaline–fuelled laugh that choked him. He had to swallow several times, trying to stifle his absurd reaction with a cough. He felt the blood drain from his face.

'You're young and otherwise in good shape, Sam, and so it could be years before you feel any more symptoms. We'll need to do some more tests but I'm going to give you these...'

He handed Sam a pile of leaflets and a book called 'Living with MS'.

'... and I will let you go home and give you some time to digest everything. Once you've read through this lot then come and see me again and I'll try to answer any questions you might have. Okay?'

Sam found himself saying, 'Yes, okay, thank you,' and shaking the doctor's hand.

As they got to the door, Dr Longford put his hand on Sam's shoulder, saying, 'I know this is no consolation but you've been lucky. Many people go months or even years without getting a diagnosis. I had just had a patient who was finally diagnosed with MS earlier this year so when you presented with similar symptoms, I sent you for the tests right away.'

'Thank you,' Sam said again, feeling anything other than grateful. He began to walk out.

'And Sam?'

Sam stopped.

'There is information there about support groups and people you can talk to. I strongly urge you to do that.'

'Thank you,' was the only word Sam could think of before he walked away in a surreal, numbed daze.

Chapter 5

Beth, Friday Afternoon

The video was just as Beth had feared: too long, too fast-paced, and with a voice-over that described the waxing process while helpful pictures flashed up, meaning that Becky needed to watch Beth's signing and the video simultaneously. Beth had to decide when it was important to sign and when it was best to just let Becky watch the screen. Once the pictures were finished, she sometimes found herself with great chunks of information to remember and then relay to Becky. She was so mentally exhausted by it all that she couldn't really remember the rest of the day. There had been writing activities and a question and answer session but she couldn't tell if any of her signing had made sense to Becky or if the girl was even engaged in the lesson. All she was thinking about was going home, taking a quick shower and then heading to the pub. Why was everything so unbearable?

When the bell rang for the end of the day, Beth walked out of the classroom without even catching Becky's eye. She almost ran to her car, jumped behind the wheel and drove away. She did get caught in traffic, but even sitting bumper to bumper beat spending one more minute in that shit-hole. On the radio was some panel show, whose presenters seemed to be competing to be the most moronic. She didn't really care and left it on, preferring noise to silence.

By the time she pulled up outside her house, her head was buzzing and she needed a drink very badly. The last thing she felt like now, though, was going out, and she was on the verge of cancelling her evening plans. She'd rather get a bottle out of the fridge, put on her pyjamas and curl up on the sofa in the safe seclusion of her home.

Just as she was about to text to cancel, her phone rang. It was flashing *Dad*. It wasn't Christmas or her birthday: why the hell would he call? He'd never been one to talk on the phone and only had a mobile because his now wife had insisted on it, so she could get hold of him when her then–husband was out for a few hours.

19

'Dad?'

'How did you know?' His voice sounded jaded. There were banging noises that sounded like several pairs of running feet echoing in the background.

'Your number's in my phone, it tells…'

'Oh yes, they do that.' And then in the same breath, he said, 'Congratulations, you've got a sister.' She could imagine him having rehearsed that line over and over until he braced himself to pick up the phone and dial her number.

'You what?'

'Vivien gave birth last night.'

'You've had a baby?'

'No, no, not me no, Vivien.'

'Yes, but it's yours, right?'

'Yes, yes, course it is.'

Beth fought to stay somewhere near calm. The ringing in her head was getting louder. 'So she's been pregnant for nine months and you somehow never got round to telling me? Oh I forgot, Christmas was nine and a half months ago and it's not my birthday until next week.'

'You never ring me.' Her dad said defensively.

'Because you asked me not to.'

'I hate phones.'

'Dad, don't you think it's the sort of thing you might make an exception for?'

'I am making an exception, it's not Christmas…'

Beth couldn't deal with this now. Her head began to feel woozy and she had to reach out for the wall and wait for it to pass. She saw stars momentarily as the fainting spell washed over her. 'Dad, I really can't talk about this now, I need to go out.'

'You're going out?' He put the emphasis on 'you're'.

'I'll call you tomorrow,' she said in a rush, pressing the END CALL button and throwing the phone on the carpeted floor in totally baffled, frustrated anger.

She suddenly had an image of her dad striding across a field with a map in a plastic wallet round his neck, one arm slung round the waist of her laughing mum. It seemed so long since all that family happiness and she was struck by just how much the man her dad had been had disappeared; to her, at least. She could wait no longer for a drink and an evening spent alone in the house had lost its appeal after all. Too many memories. She picked up her phone from the floor, grabbed her bag from the table, and headed out the door.

Chapter 6

Most of the tables in the Miller's Arms seemed to be taken by single men staring into their pints. She was forty minutes early, but didn't care. She went straight to the bar and was greeted by John, the affable landlord, whose shirt buttons strained slightly over his ever-expanding gut.

'Alright, Beth, white wine is it?' She ordered a bottle and two glasses, secretly hoping that Rick would have beer.

'Ooh, meeting someone are you? About time you got yourself a fella.'

She gave what she hoped was an enigmatic smile, but was probably more of a withered grimace, then covered it by ordering a bowl of chips to go with the wine; she needed something in her stomach before devouring this bottle.

Beth liked this place. A bottle of wine was cheap, for a pub, and it was fairly decent too. She got a booth at the side, where it was darker and quieter, and poured herself a glass. The first few mouthfuls were the best and her head started to relax. She took another couple of swigs and got her phone out to send Rick a text so he could find her.

In pub now, got a booth

By the time Rick texted back, *leaving home now 15 mins*, she was reaching for the bottle to refill her glass.

After an age, John brought the chips over with a couple of sachets of ketchup on the side, and a knife and fork wrapped in a cheap, white, paper napkin.

'Late is he?' He asked as she picked up the ketchup.

'No, he's on his way.' She tried that smile again.

John got the message and went back to the bar. The sachet of ketchup wouldn't open; in the end, she got the corner off with her teeth, squirting ketchup on her jeans.

'Oh fuck,' she growled.

'I've heard better greetings.' Rick's voice came from just by her shoulder. 'Rick! I just...' She looked down at her thigh and Rick's eyes followed her gaze.

'Give us a hug,' he said.

As they came apart and sat down, Beth said, 'I started the wine; got you a glass, although you're more of a beer man. So have what you want,' she encouraged him.

'Well, I might as well join you, this'll do me.' He sat down opposite. He might have seen a shadow of disappointment cross her face, because he added: 'We can always buy another bottle, next one's on me.' He took a chip from the bowl and poured his glass, emptying the bottle. 'Looks like we need one already. You've been here a while then?'

'Long enough.'

'You alright, Beth?'

'Why does everyone keep asking me that? Do I not look alright?'

'Not really. You look bloody knackered and fucked off.'

'Thanks.'

'Well, last time I saw you, you were full of beans about starting your dream job. I thought you were on your way to turning things around, but you're drinking like a demon and look worse.'

'Piss off, Rick, give it a rest will you?'

'Bad day was it?'

'Bad week more like. Make that a bad term.'

'Beth?'

'Not what I hoped, Rick. The tutors treat me like a bloody dogsbody.' She took a swig and emptied the glass. 'We need more wine. It's Friday night, let's talk about something else.'

'You can't still be depressed,' said Rick. 'It's nine years since Dan fucked off...'

'God, Rick, who said anything about Dan? My job is crap, it has nothing to do with him.'

'Right, but you had a crap job before and you didn't always look like the world was ending.'

She fumbled around for something to say that might shut him up and landed on the perfect thing.

'I just had a phone call from my dad.'

'Your *dad*?'

'He's had a baby.'

'He's had a *baby*?'

'Can you stop parroting me? I don't know anything about it. I hung up. Said I'll call back tomorrow.'

'Jesus, a *baby* at his age. Vivien must be a lot younger?'

'She is.'

'So how did they meet?'

'You know my dad moved out to Spain?'

'Yeah, this was once he was back on his feet after everything that happened with your mum?'

'You've got it,' Beth said wearily, tired of trying to explain the chaotic meltdown of her family. 'Well, he went regularly to Vivien's husband's club. She worked behind the bar and they started an affair. I don't know the details.' She shook her head, 'I came here to stop thinking about this stuff.'

She picked up the empty bottle and shook it again pointedly.

Rick obliged, and went to the bar for another bottle. He refilled her glass.

'I have news, too,' he told her. 'I got a new job.'

'About bloody time.'

'So long shite solutions, hello Bently's crocks, the best–value quality crockery on the market. Dinner plates, side plates, bowls, serving dishes, gravy boats, cups, mugs, milk jugs, all your crockery needs for restaurants, cafés, bistros, you name it. Started last week.'

'You've started already?! Why didn't you tell me?'

'I haven't seen you. Anyway, I wanted to see your face.'

'And how's my face?' She asked, framing it with her hands.

'Beautiful as ever,' he said, looking at her intently. Beth held his gaze for a moment and felt the tell-tale yearnings in her belly. She broke eye contact and looked at his face. A few jowls, hairline three inches further back than when she first knew him, bit of a beer belly but, otherwise, the same Rick. Shaved hair, a bit of stubble, thin lips that always seemed to be turning up at the corners.

He sighed and faintly shook his head, conspicuously ignoring the charged atmosphere.

'You were there too long, Rick,' she said, moving the moment on. 'Here's to crock-of-shit or whatever it's called.'

'Cheers,' he said, downing his glass in tandem with her.

Toward the end of the third bottle, Beth headed for the loo, self-consciously trying to look sober, waving at John with an air of dignified solemnity. The loos were small and ancient; she had to manoeuvre round the door and then pull down her jeans and knickers in one move. She sighed as she sat down.

Not Rick, she chided herself, don't do this with Rick. Rick is Rick, an old and valued mate. He's married to Claire and father to Paul and Jake. But whatever she told herself, that feeling was still present: accelerated breathing, excited queasiness. Had he taken note of it, that look?

No, Beth, she thought. 'No, Beth,' she whispered out loud, for added emphasis.

Having struggled out of the cubicle, she ran the cold tap, splashed her face and neck, and took a deep breath. In the mirror, she saw a pair of grey eyes staring back. Not the big absorbing windows to her soul that Dan had seen, but the weary, red-rimmed ones that Rick saw. Her hair was still mousy (dark blonde, Dan had insisted), in the same shoulder–length cut she'd had for years, but now it looked lank, and greasy at the roots.

'Beautiful,' she told her reflection.

Rick had poured her another glass. 'More chips or anything?'

'Nah, I'm alright.'

'Are you?'

'Rick!'

'How's your love life?'

'Rick…'

'Come on Beth, we're on our third bottle, this is what mates talk about down the pisser.'

Had he used 'mates' deliberately?

'What about Claire, how's she?'

'Avoiding the question again, I see. Claire's okay, we've been married 24 years, that's a long time to live with the same person. You know, we're okay, I'm not sure we'll last once Jake goes.'

'Oh.' She didn't know what to say to that. 'Sorry,' she mumbled to her glass.

'Don't be, that's life. We've had a good stretch, she's a good girl but it's not really human nature to spend a life with one bird.'

'I don't have a love life,' she burst out.

'Really? I can't believe that!'

'I have a sex life, Rick, but not a love one.'

'Well, everyone has a sex life. You usually know very little about people's sex lives, until you get them down the pisser of course.'

She laughed.

'My God, Beth is laughing!'

'Piss off.'

'I haven't heard you laugh properly for years. So, this sex life of yours, is it any good?'

She gave him a *for god's sake you idiot* look.

'Well, are you happy with it?'

'Yes,' she answered automatically, but then thought about it. 'Sometimes.'

'How does that work?' he coaxed.

'Online,' she offered as if that answered his question.

She couldn't remember exactly how the conversation went after that. She may or may not have told him about the ease of it, the addiction she was starting to feel to *nostrings.com*. The agreement between users not to ask any questions, to always use condoms, not to stay overnight with each other or to see anyone from the site more than once. The odd kind of camaraderie she felt with strangers who recognised a basic human need. She may have mentioned the euphoria she sometimes felt after sex and the strange hollow feeling at other times.

'So, do you approach blokes or do they ask you?'

'Either, it depends.' She pinched the bridge of her nose, regretting having started this. Rick shifted in his seat.

'You're shocked.'

'No. I'm turned on, to be honest, 'cos I'm a bloke. Look, like I say, we know nothing about most people's sex lives. Good for you, Beth

– as long as you're happy. But you don't look like a woman who's having a ball.'

'I think we need to get home,' she slurred, suddenly very, very tired of this conversation. She stood up unsteadily and took the arm he offered her.

'I'll walk you home.'

Chapter 7

Beth, Saturday Morning

Beth woke with a start and sat up. She HAD to have a drink of water. Her throat was so dry she couldn't swallow; her skin was itchy. Taking a few slugs out of the cup by her bed, she reached for the bottle of Nivea she kept on the night table. The whole of her body needed moisture; her feet were the worst, they were tingling and parched. She doused her entire body with the lotion.

After that, she drained the mug, sloshing water on her naked thighs. The clock said 4.15am, and the streetlight outside the window was glowing around the edges of the blinds. Wide awake, she got up, wrapped a dressing gown around herself, and went downstairs to make tea.

Switching on the lounge light she gasped involuntarily. Rick was asleep on the sofa. Or rather, had been asleep on the sofa.

'Is it morning?'

'Technically.'

'Time?'

'About half past four.'

'Fuck.'

'Tea?'

'Might as well.'

When she went into the kitchen to boil the kettle, she heard Rick going upstairs and, a minute later, the flush of the toilet. Rick's in my house, she thought, and then last night started coming back. It was funny, she could clearly remember the pub, the wine bottles, the chips, the looks and the conversation: oh God, the conversation. She saw it all, right up to them standing up to leave, shouting goodbye-thank you to John. What then? It was a blur.

Here they were, she had been naked in bed, Rick was on the sofa. Suddenly she saw a flash-picture of herself hugging Rick, mouths locked together in urgent, deep, exploring kisses, her pulling at Rick's shirt – but then, nothing.

'That's better,' Rick said as he came into the kitchen. 'I needed a slash.'

'Rick...?' she tailed off but her face communicated everything she was thinking.

'We didn't shag, Beth.'

'We didn't? But my clothes...'

'You did that yourself. I got you home, we were going to have a cup of tea, or maybe a shag,' he quipped, winking, 'but after we'd had a cuddle and were getting randy, you went up to the loo and never came back. I made tea and waited a bit then came upstairs and you'd thrown off your clothes and passed out on the bed. I left you to it. It was too late to go home and I was too pissed so I helped myself to a blanket and got comfy on the sofa.'

Beth reached for a couple of mugs from the draining board and dropped teabags into them.

'Why have you still got Dan's shirt in your wardrobe?' Rick asked and she flinched.

'You've been in my wardrobe?'

'I was looking for a blanket. Answer the question, Beth.'

'Can you get the milk out the fridge?'

'Beth!'

'It's the shirt he wore on our first date.'

'Right, and? Why do you have it in your wardrobe *now*? He. Fucked. Off.'

'It's not as black and white as all that. I loved him, we were in love. I still don't know where he is.'

'But the police told you, it happens all the time, blokes run off. He wasn't kidnapped, he left you a note, he knew what he was doing. They wouldn't even investigate. Open and shut, they said.'

'Yes, but...'

'But nothing, Beth. I bet he's living in Solihull with a wife called Julia who photographs fucking celebrities for a living.'

'But we don't KNOW that. Rick, we were happy.'

'Were you? Didn't you tell me he went funny?'

'He had a few weeks...'

'What about the time you rang him at work and he wasn't there?'

'Will you let me finish a sentence, Rick?' Beth asked in exasperation. 'Nobody knows where he was when I rang him at work. It happened once. Now sorry but I'm going to take this upstairs.' She held up her mug.

'Don't suppose there's any room in your bed?' He fluttered his eyelashes and tipped his head to one side.

'Don't push it.'

'Okay, okay, look, I think I'll drink this and then go home. I'll be okay to get the car from the pub and drive back now. Roads'll be deserted and, if I get lucky, Claire might not notice the time when I crawl into bed.'

Beth doubted it but said nothing, her eyes prickling.

'Stop after two bottles of wine between us next time, hey?'

She hugged him with her free arm and kissed his cheek. 'I'll text you.'

When she woke next it was 10.36am and daylight framed the blinds.

Shit was her first thought. She picked up her handset and speed–dialled the college. It rang and rang and then switched to voicemail. Belatedly, she realised that it was Saturday and she wasn't doing anything until meeting Paula at 2pm. She felt confused and disorientated.

She got up to make some more tea and found a note from Rick on the table in the hall.

I will get in your knickers one day

She found herself smiling for once, but she was thinking about Dan. His dark hair that stuck up in the mornings. His grin that gave him a little dimple every time he smiled. She'd noticed these things about him the first time she had seen him in the café at Marks and Spencer. They were both out shopping. She had wanted a new winter coat; she'd imagined him in the food halls, choosing olives and a good bottle of Sauvignon to take to his girlfriend's. They hadn't talked then, but he caught her staring at him and smiled his gorgeous smile.

She had bumped into him again later when they were queuing to pay.

'Nice gloves,' she remembered saying, nodding toward the brown leather ladies' gloves in his hands. 'For your girlfriend?'

'No, my mum, she's 65 tomorrow.' There was a slight pause. 'Nice coat,' he'd said, nodding to the functional black anorak she was holding.

'Oh yes, height of fashion, this.'

After they'd paid and she was walking away, wondering if there was any way she could manage to talk to him again, she had felt a tug on her arm. 'You forgot your bank card, it was still in the little reader thing.'

'Oh God yes, miles away!' she'd chortled.

He handed her the card, smiling and laughing, and briefly touched her arm before excusing himself and rushing off. He'd wrapped it in a sheet of paper; she had thought nothing of it at the time but, after he'd gone, she went to put the card in her purse and saw he'd written his phone number on it.

I'm Dan, call me if you fancy a drink

She still had that note, and had written the date on the back: 2 October 1999.

'Dan!' she said out loud into the silent house, 'Where the fuck are you?'

Chapter 8

1991

Beth's school had let her have the afternoon off to enter the competition. Her family arrived early and they sat on a bench outside the church drinking metallic-tasting tea from a flask Mum had brought.

'Are you nervous, maestro?' Tom asked, digging her in the ribs.

'Yes! I feel like everyone is going to be a hundred times better than me. They probably all have grade 8 and will be on BBC Young Musician of the Year 1992.'

'Your teacher wouldn't have entered you if she didn't think you had a chance,' Mum said sensibly, reaching out and taking Beth's hand.

'Exactly, the teacher would know that this competition only attracts rubbish pianists like Beth.'

'Tom! I've always hated you!'

'Now now, children, play nicely.' Dad grabbed Beth, pinning her arms to her sides. 'Just ignore him, Beth, he's only jealous.'

Tom grunted and Mum got up. 'Let's go and find our seats,' she said, and they trooped behind her, as they always seemed to do. Dad sometimes called her 'Mother Duck'.

The cavernous church was cold and there was only a smattering of people in the front four pews. Beth's family sat in the second row and looked keenly at the programme.

'Arghh, I'm first to go!' Beth said rather too loudly, sending echoes bouncing around the walls. She wished she'd been to the loo after that tea, but it was too late now.

'You'll be great and at least you can get it over with and relax. Remember, we have a surprise planned for later.' Mum squeezed her hand again reassuringly.

Beth's stomach was churning. She looked up at the beautiful stained-glass window behind the altar and said a little prayer to a God she was dubious about.

An old man in a brown suit came to the platform to welcome

everyone and then read out her name, looking round to see which of the nervous–looking young people was Beth.

Mum squeezed her arm and gently pushed her out of the pew. She felt herself shaking slightly as she went to sit at the piano and paused before she began to play, temporarily forgetting every note of the music. Once she started to play, she felt alright, concentrating on her fingers. Despite her family's admiration, she knew that she was no prodigy, never destined to be a concert musician. This was a grade 6 piece although she only had 5, really. She played okay. At least she got all the notes right and didn't miss any keys.

She sat down next to the beaming row of her three favourite people, feeling exhausted. Listening to the others play, some of them made such sonorous music that she knew she wasn't going to get any prizes.

When the pianists had all performed, the old man got back on the platform to announce the results. Beth was no longer nervous and nor did she really care what he said.

Beth was seventh out of eight competitors. She just felt relieved it was all over.

'Well done, love, you did it!'

'Our little star,' Dad said, looking very proud.

'You managed not to be last!' was Tom's offering.

'So what's the surprise?' Beth had been waiting all day.

'First, we are going for tea at Hendon's and then we are doing something else.'

'Hendon's hotel?! Wow, how posh! What is "something else"?'

'Wait and see.'

'Oh Mu-um.'

After a tea of crumpets, and more cakes than even Tom could eat, Dad put a blindfold over Beth's eyes and took her arm. They walked for what felt like a couple of streets, giggling when Beth tripped on the pavement.

'Ta-dah!' exclaimed Dad, throwing off the blindfold.

Beth looked up. They were outside a huge concert hall, facing a poster announcing a performance of Rachmaninoff's Piano Concerto Number 2.

'No way! My favourite–ever piece of music!'

Everyone was grinning.

'We were so lucky with it being on today and we got great seats!'

Beth went to hug first Mum and then Dad, before grabbing Tom's arm and pulling him toward the building. She would remember this day forever.

Chapter 9

Sam, 2007

'You wanted to see me?' Sam said to Brian Crosby, his supervisor, as he knocked on his open door.

'Ah, Sam, yes, come in, come in. Take a seat.'

Sam sat on the proffered chair, holding his breath in an irrational attempt to prevent Crosby from speaking further.

'Can Sharon get you tea? Coffee? Water?'

'No, nothing for me thanks.' He was just waiting for the words he'd been expecting for the last few months. Words which seemed more inevitable after the diagnosis last month, even though nobody at work knew about that yet.

'Well, Sam, I won't beat around the bush but it's hard for me to know how to put this.'

Here it comes, Sam thought.

'You are a good worker, Sam, and people here seem to really like you. I used to get requests for you to be part of a particular team.'

'You used to, right.'

'In the last few months, though, I've had one or two reports that you seem to be struggling a bit.' Crosby looked at Sam, waiting for an explanation but he wasn't ready to give one yet.

'So, are you struggling, Sam? I understand you and your wife had a baby not long ago? Is it that? Sleepless nights?'

Sam breathed in and out before he spoke. 'Kim's not my wife but yes, we have a baby. He's over a year old now.'

'Ah, wearing you out is he?'

'Erm…' Sam just wanted him to say it. 'Do you need to let me go or…?'

'Let you go?! No, Sam, but I need to know what's going on and why your performance is flagging. Once I know that, we can see what we can do. If it's the baby, everything will get back to normal soon, once he gets into his routines.'

'Erm, well', Sam rubbed his temples before continuing: he knew he had to come out and say it, 'I've got multiple sclerosis.'

There was a pause, like Crosby wasn't sure what to say.

'You might know it just as MS.'

'I've heard of it. So how long will it be before you're better?'

Sam felt odd now that he'd said it. For the past three or four weeks, since the diagnosis, he hadn't told a soul, not even Kim. He found that if he didn't tell anyone, he didn't have to deal with it because it wasn't an issue in his life. The problem was that it *was* an issue and it *was* affecting him.

He had skimmed over the leaflets from the doctor, seeing words like *progressive* and *lifelong*, with lists of possible symptoms like vision problems, mobility difficulties, loss of bladder control, muscle spasms, not to mention reduced life expectancy.

Granted, some of these he was feeling now: the loss of coordination, the muscle fatigue and so on he knew were due to his MS, but somehow, by not talking about it, he could still carry on as if none of the rest of it was going to happen to him.

'Sam?' Crosby brought him back to the room. 'Will it take long to get better?'

Sam sighed. 'It's not going to get better, Brian, MS is a permanent thing. I've got some leaflets about it in my locker, you can read them if you like.'

'Right, I will. Look, Sam,' he hesitated, 'we're worried you're going to do yourself harm or put other people in danger.'

Sam went cold.

'We need someone to join the fire prevention team and I thought of you. You're good with the public.' He said it as if 'the public' had a capital 'P'.

'Going round people's houses and checking their toasters aren't going to spark, you mean?'

'Not just that Sam, it's a vital role. Checking and installing alarms, looking for fire hazards. So many fires could be avoided in the first place. You'd be saving more lives than you are now and you wouldn't have to pull any dead babies out of a blaze.'

'Right then, okay.'

'I mean it, Sam, it's a very rewarding thing to do. Go and have a cup of tea and think it over then we'll talk business.'

'Right, well, thanks.'

'And get me those leaflets.'

As soon as Sam pulled up outside their terraced house, knowing that he couldn't put off telling Kim any longer, she ran out of the door waving a letter.

'Sam, you're not going to believe this!'

'What?' he asked dutifully.

'Uncle Julian has left me £50,000!'

He noted the 'me' instead of 'us'.

'It means I can get an au pair to look after Ollie for me.'

'An au pair?'

'I found one online already. She's a German girl called Greta and the agency have forwarded my details to her to check she'd like the job. I picked the cutest photo of Ollie wearing his teddy–bear suit looking like a cherub, you'd never guess what a terror he can be.'

Sam wasn't going to argue. It was her money and an extra pair of hands around the house would definitely make things easier.

'That's great,' he said, wondering how on earth he was going to tell her now. On second thoughts, was now the perfect time, when she was so fired up about the money?

He put his arm round her minuscule waist, but she pulled away slightly in a move that was so subtle it was barely noticeable; but Sam felt it. He knew how easily she used to sink into his embrace and it made him swallow his words again.

They went indoors and Sam went up to see Ollie, who was sleeping peacefully in his cot. He stood there calming himself for a while, gently stroking Ollie's rosy cheek and trying to absorb some of his strife-free slumber. His head was spinning. He needed someone to talk to but Kim had never been that person. She seemed unable to allow life to be anything other than handbags and glad rags.

With heavy heart, he went to find Kim, resolved to tell her. She was on the phone but hung up as soon as he entered the room. He'd noticed her doing this more frequently recently.

'Is he still asleep?' she asked, sounding slightly breathless and look-ing flushed.

'Yes, away with the fairies.'

'That's good.'

There was an awkwardness he never used to feel. Was she seeing someone else?

'Look, Kim, I need to tell you something.' He sat next to her on the sofa.

'Are you seeing someone else, Sam?'

'Me?! God no, Kim! Why do you say that?'

'I don't feel like this is working out any more.'

Sam just looked at her.

'Plus, you keep looking at me like that.'

'How do I look at you?'

'Like I disappoint you. I haven't changed, Sam, you have, you just seem so serious recently, so, well, dull.'

'That word again.' He swallowed. To be honest, he'd seen this coming a long time now. If Kim was seeing someone else, it would be just like her to hope that Sam was so that she wouldn't have to be the culpable one. He wasn't going to ask now – it was unlikely he'd get the truth anyway. Whether Kim realised it or not, she was a game-player.

'So you're saying you want a break?' he asked instead.

'I'm saying I'm not sure how I feel about you any more. You've changed, Sam. You used to be such a charmer, so much fun, my friends all envied me.'

'And now?'

'Now, they think I'm trapped, they feel sorry for me.'

'It's called growing up, Kim.'

'It's called becoming boring. Who wants to be old? Now I've got this money, I don't have to be trapped any more.'

'I can't believe this conversation. It feels like déjà vu.' Sam got up.

'Where are you going?'

'Out. I need to get my head round what you're saying. There's a lot I need to get my head round.'

'Go then.'

As he reached the door, she seemed to remember that he'd wanted to tell her something. 'What was it you wanted to tell me?'

'Forget it, it's not important.' He couldn't bear to tell her now, couldn't bear to see her grappling to deal with it. His fear was that she wouldn't even try to deal with it.

Sam felt that everything was spinning out of control. Surely it wasn't possible for his world to shatter any further?

Chapter 10

Beth, Saturday Afternoon

At two on the dot, Beth pulled up outside Paula's. She was feeling nervous, unsure she'd done the right thing in agreeing to this job. Paula had said they could give it a few weeks' trial period, which she claimed was for both herself and Beth, but Beth had the feeling that she would be the one under scrutiny.

She sat in the car for a while, and cleared sweet wrappers off the passenger seat. Paula's house was a modern detached, not cheap round here. Her partner Donna's car wasn't in the driveway; she coached a football team, Beth knew, so was sure to be at a match this afternoon.

Already a bit late, she forced herself out and walked over the gravel forecourt to the house. She knew it quite well from when Paula had been her BSL teacher and run classes from a room she'd converted for the purpose. There was no sound when she rang the bell but she knew that Paula would have her pager on. She had a wristband that vibrated and flashed to tell her when the doorbell was ringing.

Beth heard barking from Paula's dog, Barney, and the faint clump–clump of someone coming slowly down the stairs.

At last, the door opened.

Hello, signed Paula. *How are you?*

They hugged slightly awkwardly. Beth wasn't sure if she should do this, but Paula opened her arms to her.

Sorry I'm a bit late. What's the plan for today? Beth signed, making sure that she was visible in Paula's limited field of vision.

I need to go shopping, I've got a jumper to take back to Fornby's.

43

Sounds good. Drive or bus?
Let's go in the car. I'll get Barney.

Barney was a chocolate lab assistance dog, trained not only as a guide dog but a hearing dog too. He was the calmest, wisest dog that Beth had ever met, and vital to Paula.

When they got into town, Beth found a parking place on some double yellow lines, thanks to Paula's blue parking badge. They got everything out of the car, put Barney's assistance dog coat on, and headed straight for Fornby's, an old-fashioned store hanging on in a row of UK-wide ubiquitous high-street chains.

The lady behind the returns desk was in her fifties, with shoul-der-length grey hair and an elegant black-and-grey-striped silk scarf tied over her obligatory black skirt suit.

'Good afternoon, how can I help you?' she enquired, looking at Beth.

'Paula is the customer today,' Beth said curtly, already feeling some of Paula's frustration at always being bypassed.

How can she help? She signed to Paula.

Paula pulled a soft chenille jumper from her Fornby's bag.

> *This is too small. I want my money back*, she signed, looking at the woman, who looked at Beth with a hint of pity in her eyes.

'She says, the jumper's too small, can she have a refund?'

'We don't do refunds unless the garment is faulty, but I will gladly change it for a larger size.'

Beth signed this to Paula.

> *I don't want another one, just the money back.*

'She says she doesn't want a replacement, but would like a refund.'

'I'm sorry but we don't do refunds,' she repeated. 'I could give her a voucher to choose a similar-priced garment another time.'

Beth signed this to Paula, nodding her head in an attempt to tell her that this was a good deal but Paula signed:

I want the money back.

'She says could she have it refunded?' Beth felt flustered but remembered something she'd been taught on the Usher syndrome awareness course that Paula had sent her on: a person guiding a deaf-blind adult was a conduit, that's the word they'd used – it meant being someone's eyes and ears and helping with communication but not, definitely not, taking over decisions or talking for them. Paula was a grown woman and Beth was not here to judge or decide what she should say.

'I'm sorry, but that's not our policy.'

Beth signed to Paula, holding her breath. Paula signed back:

But I'm deaf-blind.

Beth felt hot now, awkward. 'She says she'd like the money back because she is deaf-blind.' She could feel herself blushing involuntarily and took care to make it plain that it was Paula saying this, not her. If Paula chose not to explain why a deaf-blind person may find it harder to shop for the right size then she wasn't going to say it for her.

The lady behind the counter was by now looking flustered and angry too. Possibly, just to make things easier, she took the decision to give Paula her refund. Paula accepted it with barely a smile and took Beth's arm as she turned to walk away.

Coffee? Beth asked her hopefully.
Yes please.

As on previous occasions when they'd met for social coffees, Beth and Paula headed for Luigi's – officially called The Perfect Shot, but known by all as Luigi's after its flamboyant Italian owner.

'Ah, here they are!' he beamed, as if he'd been waiting for them all day. 'Two cappuccinos and a chocolate brownie to share, yes?'

Beth was impressed; that was what they'd had last time. She gently tapped Paula's arm so that she would look up, and Luigi moved into her sight line.

Good afternoon, he signed, in the way that Paula had taught him.

Good afternoon, Paula smiled. Beth knew that it made a great difference to Paula when people learned just a few signs, and she always tried to explain to people she met regularly the best way for them to communicate. Luigi was a natural, with none of the awkwardness that people often seemed to have around Paula.

Beth took Barney's lead so that he could walk in front of them and then, having positioned herself in front of Paula, who put her hands on Beth's shoulders, the two of them walked in single file through the busy café. Helpful people moved chairs out of the way, some with that annoying frozen smile of sympathy that Beth seemed to see so often when she was with Paula, a look she was glad that Paula herself probably missed.

Beth found some free seats and arranged them so that Paula was looking directly at her. Barney lay down calmly under the table.

When the coffees arrived, together with the brownie, already halved and on two plates, Paula signed:

I have something to ask you.
What?
Donna and I have booked to go on a horse–riding break next weekend…
Great.
… But Donna can't make it now as the football team she coaches got through to the cup final. She needs to be here for them. We didn't think they'd get through…

Oh, that's great for the team but a shame for you.

… So I was wondering, Paula continued in rapid signing,*if you could come on the holiday as my PA? It's all paid for and you work on a Saturday anyway so you can work less hours for a few weeks afterwards to get back the hours you're owed.*

Horse riding?

Yes, RDA: I go locally once a week. But this is a riding week-end in the Lakes.

It should be fine. Hang on, let me check…

Beth scrolled through her handset and brought up her e-diary, although she already knew she had nothing on. In fact, she'd love to be busy over her birthday weekend.

Yes, I'm free. It was too late now, she'd said it, so the doubts she knew she'd have would need to be ignored. *I've never ridden a horse.*

Well, you can always walk with us instead of riding or not come on the treks at all.

Would you need me on the treks for communication?

Probably not when we're riding; me and Donna have been before. The couple who run the place didn't sign then but we taught them a little and they try very hard. It was brilliant there. It said beginners welcome so you might find you like riding if you try it. You never know.

Beth sincerely doubted it, but Paula was still signing fast and was looking excited:

Great, thank you. Donna will be pleased as she was worried it would mean I would miss it too.

Beth felt glad to help, and glad to have been asked: it meant that Paula must have accepted her.

Chapter 11

Beth, Saturday Evening

Although exhausted by the time she got home, Beth was buoyed up by the sense that Paula really did have trust in her.

It was only after food and a few glasses of wine that she felt ready to ring her dad. His mobile was switched off so she tried the landline number.

On the fifth ring, a woman picked up.

'Si?'

'Vivien? It's me.' Talking to Vivien wasn't the plan so the only thing Beth could think to say was 'congratulations'.

'Who is this?'

'It's Beth.'

There was a pause but Beth could hear whispering.

'Is my dad there?'

'Yes... erm... I mean no... he's gone out.' Beth heard more rustling, which could have been the sound of someone scribbling notes.

'Will he be long?'

'I don't know, Beth. Sorry, the baby's crying, I'll have to go. I'll ask your dad to ring you.'

Beth strained to hear a baby's cries but failed to hear anything except what sounded like her dad, shushing it.

She hung up and tasted bile in her mouth. How could she have been so stupid as to think anything other than that would happen?

So much for feeling on top of things – how could she when the world was so much against her? As if to reinforce her feelings of use-lessness and inadequacy, the TV news headlines were announcing war, bombs, debt crisis and poverty. Suddenly, everything was closing in on her again and tears were pricking her eyes.

Fighting to stay in control, she searched for something, anything, to keep her from falling into the familiar pit of despair. Her mind brought her back to Paula and her promise to email details of the riding holiday.

Even that thought made her stomach turn over. Why in hell had she agreed to it so glibly?

She did switch on her laptop, though: perhaps photos of the place would help?

There was no email from Paula but there was one from *nostrings*.

Exciting news!! Billybear sent you a message at 17.45!

Logging into the site she read:

Hello Sweetmusic, let's make sweet music! Xx

It was getting on for seven, but she typed hurriedly:

Are you there Billybear? x

She already felt her stomach twist and the powerful surge of wanting.

Waiting, and desperately hoping that he was still around, she scrolled through his profile, learning little, other than his love of pizza, holding hands and snuggling in front of the TV.

A message pinged:

Hi Sweetmusic!! Yes I am here! Waiting for you! Do you want me? Xx

Yes.

Then you can have me! What is your address?? xx

She gave it to him blithely.

See you in 20! Xxxxxxxxxx

And that was that. Beth ran upstairs to change and clean her teeth. Just as she was wiping toothpaste from her chest the doorbell rang. *Billybear* looked much like his profile picture, which was a nice change from most of the men she met this way.

He came in and closed the door.

'Are we alone?' he asked, as if expecting otherwise.

'Yes.'

'Good.'

He reached for her immediately and they started to kiss. His lips were cold at first and he bit her lip slightly.

'Upstairs!' He whispered urgently, already fumbling for his belt. 'Get upstairs.'

When she fell on her bed he pulled off her trousers and knickers and began to kiss the inside of her ankles; licking, biting and kissing his way up her calves, her thighs and finally, finally between her legs.

'Do you like this, Sweetmusic? Do you? Do you? Do you want more? Shall I give it to you? Do you want it from Daddy? Ask Daddy!'

Beth was too far gone to feel anything but lust – what he was doing was glorious.

'Yes!' she said.

'Yes what?'

'I want more. Please!'

'Ask Daddy!'

His fingers replaced his tongue as he crawled next to her on the bed and deftly put on a condom with his other hand.

'Do you want it? Say it! Ask Daddy!'

'Please, Daddy!'

With that, he flipped her over, pulled her on to all fours and fucked her. There was no other word for it.

When she came round, he was just getting dressed.

'I have to go.'

'Back to your wife?'

He shook his head in refusal to answer.

'No strings, remember? You know, you should be more careful about who you invite to your house.'

He left then, kissing her gently on her forehead. She wondered if anyone would ever understand what she'd just done.

She took a shower and stood with the hot water pounding her head and running down her face. She had an odd feeling of euphoria, tempered by one of disgust and self–loathing. Fortunately for her, the whole *nostrings* thing felt slightly surreal: she was just playing the role of Sweetmusic. No one knew about it, which increased the feeling of otherworldliness.

With no idea how long she'd been standing in the shower, she was roused by the sound of her phone ringing. No one ever called her on her landline.

She quickly got out from under the water and pulled a towel round herself, running downstairs.

'Hello?'

'Finally, I thought you must be out. Why did you ring me?'

'Dad? I didn't think you'd call back.'

'Vivien said I should ring you.'

'Ah, I see, Vivien said.'

Her heart was sinking already.

'Why did you phone me?'

Beth was finding it hard to form any coherent thoughts, but after a moment it all came back to her. 'Yesterday, you told me I have a half-sister. I thought it might be nice to know her name.'

'Lucy.'

'And is Lucy pretty?'

'She's a baby!' he scoffed, as if she was an idiot for suggesting that a baby might have characteristics.

'Are you having her christened?'

'Vivien wants a welcome party and baby greeting.' He sounded derisive.

'Right, is that like a christening?' She felt slightly nauseous and muddle-headed.

'No church. A lot of cooing, photos, presents, that kind of thing.'

'And when will it be?' she asked, trying and failing to calculate how to get there.

'Next Saturday.'

'Next Saturday?! I'm working, I can't possibly get out to Spain.'

'It's for friends and family,' he said in a monotone voice.

'Yes, family, *Dad.*' She put the emphasis on *Dad.*

'Vivien's family.' He countered immediately.

'Please, Daddy!' she said, before she knew what she was doing.

There was silence down the line and Beth dropped the phone with a cry, as if she were touching burning hot coals. Her mind was whirling: there was *Billybear*, and then images of her dad holding her hand as a child, blowing raspberries on her stomach as he dried her after a bath.

He became Dan, stroking her arm in an empty cinema, kneading her sore shoulders as she sat and watched TV, sticking out his tongue in concentration as he fixed a broken vase. *Oh God!*

She must have made it to the sofa before blanking out and then waking in darkness. Wine was soaking through her jumper where she'd let a glass slip out of her hands. The clock on her phone showed 1.15am. Feeling totally unable to go up to bed, all she could think to do was to idly log back into *nostrings*. The only person currently online and available in her area was *Rockman*. She barely glanced at his profile, just asked him to come, not even bothering to change out of her wine-damp clothes.

Standing in her hall, he looked at least 15 years older than his photo: stocky, rough, needing a shave. They went upstairs in silence and sat side by side on the bed, taking off their own clothes before they'd even hugged or spoken. In the chill, Beth climbed under the covers and he rolled on top of her, his solid, heavy bulk pinning her down. He was looking into the pillows, not once meeting her eyes, and started grunting, thrusting into her and holding her arms by her sides so that she couldn't even move. Minutes later he rolled off, wiping the spittle from his chin, and put his clothes back on.

'Thanks, love,' he said, 'I'll see myself out.' These were the first words he'd spoken since he arrived.

She lay in the bed with the covers over her head and sobbed. What the hell was she doing? Could she go any lower than this?

Chapter 12

'It's like when you didn't even tell me about your MS until after we broke up!' Kim shouted.

They were sitting in the lounge of his recently acquired new flat and Kim was pointing at the cast on Sam's arm. Ollie was playing happily with his cars at their feet.

'I didn't tell you about my MS because it wouldn't have made any difference, you would have kicked me out anyway. I didn't tell you about this,' he held his arm up, 'because, quite frankly, why should I?' Sam already felt tired. All they seemed to do these days was wind each other up.

'Of course telling me about your MS would have made a difference, I didn't know you were ill!'

'If that's true then I'm very glad I didn't tell you. The last thing I'd have wanted was for you to stay with me because you felt sorry for me.'

'So you left it for me to hear it from Brian bloody Crosby and have to stand there in Asda pretending I knew what the fuck he was talking about?'

Sam was trying to keep his voice calm. 'If you must know, I didn't tell you straight after I saw the doctor because I needed time to process it all. Then, when I got put on fire prevention, I was going to tell you that day but came home to you dancing around and cheering about your windfall and telling me you didn't love me any more.'

He felt his jaw clenching and the cast on his arm was irritating him more than ever.

'I'm sure I didn't say that.'

'If you didn't, it was obvious that's what you meant. I also suspect that that Ernesto bloke was already in the picture.'

'His name is Enrico.'

Sam scoffed, 'So he was in the picture?'

Kim didn't say anything and Sam didn't press her, too tired to really care one way or the other. The levels of fatigue he was experiencing at the moment were crippling: he felt like he was moving through glue and very often his mind became so woolly he had to give up trying to think. He leaned back against the cushions, his broken arm aching.

'Are you managing with that arm?' she asked, changing her tone to that of concerned nurse, obviously wanting to get off the subject now that she was under scrutiny.

'Yes,' he replied. He couldn't be bothered to go into it, knowing her interest wasn't going to go beyond asking.

'Well, you're tired and I only popped in to get Ollie's cars. Look how much he loves them!'

Sam looked at his son, immersed in his world of cars. He got down on the floor to sit with him and Ollie drove a car up his leg. God, he missed this. He picked him up as best he could with one arm and Ollie drove his car down Sam's nose, oblivious to everything.

'We're going to have to talk about an arrangement so I can see more of Ollie and not just when you need a babysitter on Greta's days off.'

'Hm-mm,' was all she managed in response. Sam knew how evasive she could be about things she didn't want to talk about.

'I mean it, Kim.' He looked at her as she checked her face in her compact mirror.

He couldn't stand it that she held all the cards but he couldn't allow his anger to get the better of him, not with Ollie snuggling into his shoulder.

'We will, Sam,' she said, picking Ollie up, 'later. I have to go now.'

She walked out, leaving Sam sitting on the floor feeling completely hollowed out. He picked up the mug by his hand and flung it at the wall with all the strength he could muster.

The only thing he could think of to release some of his pent-up tension was to try having a wank. It was tricky with one arm out of action, but fortunately it was his weaker arm so he got a towel from the bathroom and sat on the bed.

Frustrated as he was, it took a long time and he tried to work through his bank of fantasies. Just as he was finally nearing release, he heard voices calling and the front door slamming.

What the hell?

'Sorry we're late, Mr Owens, our last client had a fall.'

He could hear them moving through the flat.

He fumbled with his trousers as best he could, pulling up the zip, his penis throbbing now, and with no time to do up his button before the pair of home help women got to his bedroom door.

'Ah, there you are, Mr Owens, thought you must be asleep.'

'What are you doing?' he asked incredulously.

'We've come to give you your shower,' said the eldest of them, as if he might have forgotten that they would.

'But what the hell are you doing just walking into my house?'

'We were given your key–safe number so we used that,' she said, like they'd been doing him a favour.

'But that's just for emergencies!' He was irate now. 'You can't just fucking walk in!'

'I'm sorry, Mr Owens, it won't happen again. We'll make a note in your file.'

'Yes, of course, in my *file*.' Sam was so sick of people with their files, forms, risk assessments and analyses. People invaded his life as if he was not expected to have any opinions or interests of his own any more. He knew why he was called an invalid: in-valid.

'And can you give me more idea of what time you'll come by?' He tamped down his ire.

'Sorry, we can't do that. We get given a list of clients at the start of each day and we never know how long each visit will last.'

Sam felt defeated, too exhausted to fight. Clients, he thought, clients!

'Come on, sunshine, let's get you in that shower. How did you break your arm anyway?'

Sam had explained the real story of tripping over a kerb to every single home help who'd turned up. He was *that* close to throwing these two out of the flat, feeling violated by the intrusion, but he needed a shower so instead he said, 'It was a skiing accident.'

Chapter 13

Beth and her friends hung about a bit after school, popping into town to get an iced bun from Thurstons. They'd almost-accidentally bumped into Liam, Ian, Simon and Martin, who'd been in Woolworths next door to get cans of coke and nick some pick–and–mix. 'Almost' because they'd seen the boys go into the shop and had loitered until they came out again. Not actively waiting, obviously, Beth convinced herself. When they'd met in the street, Liam had pulled out a toffee from his pocket and offered it to Beth, who'd held out a hand sticky with the sugary frosting from her bun.

'Thanks,' she smiled shyly and he grinned at her. She didn't really like toffees, so it would take pride of place on her bookshelves.

Her friend Kate had spotted this interaction and knew that Beth fancied Liam, with his dimply smile and skinny good looks. Kate said that she didn't like him at all, far too immature, but it seemed that she wanted to get things moving and was tired of the shilly-shallying.

'It's Beth's birthday tomorrow,' she said pointedly to Liam, who blushed slightly. 'We're going to the Scene on Friday, want to come?'

Beth felt herself blushing too. She got hold of Kate's arm and gently tried to pull her away. Liam was looking at his shoes, awkwardly pretending to kick something out of the way, but then he'd glanced at Beth.

'Yeah?' he questioned.

'Yeah.'

'Cool.'

Beth was buzzing: she'd been looking forward to Friday, but now it would be even better. She had already planned how she'd do her hair, which of her earrings she'd put in, which nail polish she'd use.

When she got home, there was a note from Mum saying, *Popped to*

Tesco, back by 5. It was half past four already so she put in her new Simply Red CD and switched straight to 'Stars', singing along to her favourite bit of the song and this time meaning every word.

She started dancing round her room as she changed out of her school uniform and looked out her window when she heard a car pull up. It was Mum's Honda Civic, and Beth saw her pulling out carrier bags from the boot and hauling them toward the house. She knocked on her window and Mum looked up briefly and nodded a smile.

Beth left the CD playing and went down to help unpack, and to see what food Mum had bought. The Day of Shopping, as they called it, usually meant Dairy Milks for the evening, when they were watching Inspector Morse on the telly. Mum had put four bags on the kitchen counter and had gone back to the car for one more and to shut the boot. Beth dived into the first bag.

'Don't look in those!' Mum shouted lightly when she came back in. 'There's a surprise for tomorrow.'

'Oops, sorry, do you mean this?' She pulled out a choc-nut Viennetta, her favourite.

'Oh Beth!' Mum snatched it from her and hid it behind her back, cuffing Beth in mock anger.

'What?!'

'I said not to look.'

'Look at what? I have seen nothing,' she deadpanned.

'That's better, now go away while I unpack.'

'Yes, miss.' She headed out of the room with a salute but turned back on her way out. 'What time is Tom getting here?'

'Late, I'm getting him from the station at about 9.30. Tea will be at 6. Now buzz off.'

'Buzzzz,' she retorted, flapping her hands like little wings as she headed back to her room.

She could hear her mum putting things in cupboards, and switching on Radio 4 to listen to someone talking about something boring. Luckily, when she got to her room and closed the door, there was only Mick Hucknall singing 'She's Got It Bad'. Beth lay on her bed and closed her eyes, humming along. She couldn't wait to see Tom.

Whenever she spoke to him on the phone, which wasn't all that often because they could never get hold of him and he barely ever got round to ringing home, he always seemed to be on his way out to a party. She hadn't visited him yet, but was a bit nervous of meeting his friends and looking like the little kid sister.

The front door slammed and she heard her dad shouting, 'I'm ho-ome' from the bottom of the stairs. She popped her head out of her bedroom door to say hi as he headed for the kitchen, no doubt straight for the drinks cabinet and his favourite single malt.

She heard Mum saying, 'Welcome ho-ome' and giving him a kiss before asking, 'You did remember to book the restaurant for tomorrow, didn't you?'

'Oh, shit!'

'I despair! Go and ring them now!'

It was always like that. Beth had no idea how Dad would function without her mum.

After a lamb–chop tea, during which conversation had focused mainly on plans for Beth's birthday and the questions they had for Tom, they still had an hour before Morse started at eight. Mum was going to watch the first hour and then record the second half while she went to get Tom. The station was only twenty minutes away, so they should be home by the end of it, before Beth went to bed.

'Anyone want a quick walk round the block before the telly?' Mum asked, looking mainly at Beth, as Dad never did.

'Yeah, that'd be good,' Beth clapped, and she ran off to get her coat and boots.

'You'll need gloves, it's getting chilly,' Mum shouted from the kitchen.

'I KNOW.' Beth rolled her eyes to herself.

They headed out the back door and through the garden. It was almost dark, but not quite. Beth loved twilight. She could smell autumn in the air and feel the chill on her cheeks; she was glad she'd put her scarf on. Mum was striding ahead, head bent forward.

'Slow down!' Beth ran a few steps to catch up, 'You walk so fast.'

'Time waits for no man.'

'But maybe she will wait for women?' They laughed, and Mum put her arm through Beth's as they strode along the pavement, feet in unison like three-legged runners; they laughed at that too.

'So who's going to be there on Friday?' Mum always wanted to know everything.

'Oh Kate, Jo, Lou, maybe Karen.'

'Any boys?' Mum said innocently.

'Maybe.'

'Maybe?'

'Yeah,' Beth felt herself blushing in the near darkness.

Mum looked at her and nudged her in the ribs, smiling, and left it there.

Their walk took them to the end of the road, past the park, then back home again, in a brief circuit. When they got into the warmth, Mum went to put her dressing gown on and Beth did the same. When she came back downstairs at ten to eight, Dad had the fire going in the lounge and was sitting reading the paper, sipping his scotch. Mum had already joined him at the other end of the settee, where she was doing a crossword.

'Tea?' Beth asked.

'Oh thanks, love, and bring the Dairy Milks too, can you?'

'Course.'

She made a proper pot of tea and carried it to the lounge on a tray. Dad had disappeared, no doubt to the loo: he always left it to the last second before something came on TV. When he came back in, the programme had already started, and Beth and Mum were watching in avid silence in case they missed any clues.

'I thought I'd get...' Dad started, but he was stopped abruptly by protests of 'Shhhhh, it's important.'

He went to sit down, but 'Shut the DOOR!' Beth hissed, without taking her eyes off the screen, as a draught filled the snug room.

He went back to close the door, huffing to himself, and then sat down finally. Beth was on the floor and handed him a mug of tea from the tray.

'Does it...?'

'Shhhh.'

He fell silent at last, drinking his tea despite the fact that there was no sugar in it. He probably didn't dare ask Beth to pass him the bowl.

Just before nine, there was an advert break.

'Right, I'd better go, do you want to come, Beth?'

Beth was snugly engrossed by the programme and shook her head.

'Are you sure? Your dad's recording it.'

'No, you go, it's cold out there and you'll be back by the time this finishes. Are you going like that?' she asked, indicating Mum's dressing gown.

'Yes, why not? Nobody'll see in the dark.'

'What if you have a crash?' Beth joked.

'Don't be silly, we'll be back in no time as long as the train's on time. See you.'

She went out to the hall and Beth heard her getting her car keys and going out the front door. Half a minute later, she drove away.

When the programme finished, and its melodic, hypnotic theme tune was playing, Beth automatically glanced at the clock. It was stupid: she knew it was ten because the credits were rolling. Her dad noticed.

'Train must be late,' he said. 'Give 'em fifteen minutes, otherwise I'm sure Mum will find a payphone and let us know their ETA.'

'Yeah,' Beth shrugged, standing up to take the tea tray back to the kitchen. She refilled the kettle for her hot-water bottle and put out a clean mug in case Tom wanted a hot drink. She went to the window by the front door but there was no car. Her eyes were starting to feel gritty and tired but she wanted to see Tom before bed.

Getting out the Yellow Pages, Beth looked up a number to get information about train times and tapped it out on the new keypad phone, recently purchased to replace the old dial one. She'd liked the sound the dial made and missed its whirring.

The voice at the other end asked her which train she was enquiring about and she gave the details.

'There are no reported delays on this train. Is there anything else I can help you with?'

'No, thank you,' she said, and hung up.

'The train was on time,' she called to Dad.

'Maybe Tom missed it and your mum is waiting to see if he's on the next one?'

'Yeah, maybe, but why hasn't she rung? There're loads of phones at the station.'

'Maybe they're on their way. Maybe they stopped for a quick drink?'

Beth didn't think that was very likely but she didn't say anything. It was 10.20pm now and she decided to wait at least another ten minutes, going back in the lounge and idly picking up Mum's unfinished crossword as she waited for the sound of tyres on the road or car doors slamming.

The clock ticked on to ten thirty.

'I wish I'd gone with her. I hate waiting.'

'Won't be long now, I'm sure.'

'She needs one of those phones you carry about with you.'

'God no! They're just for yuppies.'

'Dad! You're such an old man!' Beth sighed and stared at the crossword without really looking at it. There were only two clues left and she didn't know what the words meant, exactly: erudite, sequestered. Normally, she'd get out the dictionary and thesaurus but she couldn't be bothered and put the paper aside. Her thoughts were shutting down with tiredness.

'I think I'm going to have to go to bed.'

'Yeah, okay, I bet Tom will be worn out too. I might turn in myself soon.'

'Goodnight. Hopefully, they'll get here while I'm cleaning my teeth. Tell Tom to knock on my door and say hi if not.'

'Will do, you never know.'

As she came out of the bathroom, toothpaste still smudged round her mouth, she heard a car pull up outside.

'At last,' she whispered under her breath and ran to the landing window to look out. There was a police car pulled up outside and two people were getting out heading toward the front door. Beth gasped as the doorbell rang.

Her dad opened the door, by now wearing his pyjamas. He looked old and grey.

'Good evening, officers, can I help you?' He sounded stilted.

'Mr Leary?' the male officer said.

'Yes, that's me.'

'Can we go and sit down please?'

'Oh God…'

Just then the female officer looked up and saw Beth hovering at the top of the stairs.

'Hello, love?' She glanced at her partner. 'Will you make me a cup of tea while my colleague talks to your dad?'

Beth's dad glanced over. 'She's 16.'

'Not until tomorrow,' Beth muttered, stupidly.

'Well, let's put the kettle on, shall we?'

Beth came down the stairs while the men went into the lounge. She stood in front of the policewoman, who looked flushed and awkward.

'Is it my mum?' she demanded, looking the officer right in the eye.

The policewoman looked down and Beth knew then, if she hadn't known before, that it was. She felt bile rising to her throat, and a block of ice filling her chest and stopping her from breathing. Just then, they heard her dad cry out.

'Nooo!'

Beth ran to the lounge and dived at him to hold him, and be held, but he pushed her away brusquely, almost pushing her over.

'Tell me what happened,' he begged, ignoring Beth.

The police officer came over to her and put an arm around her shoulder, trying to lead her from the room.

'No, let me stay, I want to know, I need to be here.' She felt numbed suddenly, anaesthetised.

'Alright, love, what's your name?'

'Beth.'

'I'm Debbie and this is Pete, come and sit down here.' She led Beth to the sofa and sat beside her. 'Witnesses say Mrs Leary's vehicle pulled out in front of a lorry. There was nothing the driver could do. I'm sorry. They won't have suffered, they died on impact.'

Dad snorted piercingly, inhumanly.

'They?' whispered Beth, the ice creeping over her again.

'Your mum and the driver of the car, a young man – we haven't identified him yet.'

'Tom.' Beth said in monotone, sitting on her hands, dry-eyed. This was just too surreal.

'Tom?' Debbie repeated. When Beth only nodded, she asked, 'Who was Tom?'

'My brother. Mum was getting him from the train.'

Debbie looked at Pete, wide-eyed. She shook her head and turned to Beth. 'Beth,' she said gently, 'is there anyone we can call who might look after you tonight while your dad helps us out? Family, friends, neighbours?'

'Where's Dad going?'

'We'll need the bodies to be identified.'

Beth choked then, as her dad turned to leave the room silently, without being asked, and walked out of the house to the waiting police car, still in his dressing gown and slippers.

Chapter 14

Beth, Monday

Beth didn't start at college until ten. She'd slept fitfully through the night but had just gone into a deep sleep when her alarm went off, prodding her into a fug of semi-conscious confusion. She staggered to the bathroom and, already naked, stood under a blast of water. The shower head was set on massage and a thin powerful jet pummelled her sore back muscles. She stood there until she felt her brain beginning to engage. Saturday night was already feeling more like a terrible confused dream than a real event and she'd prefer it to stay that way.

With only ten minutes before she'd have to leave, she had a cup of tea for breakfast, and opened a packet of ginger-nut biscuits to go with it. Heading out, she caught sight of herself in the hall mirror. She'd started to put on weight around her face: her cheeks looked puffy and there were slight jowls framing her chin. The buttons on her grey shirt were straining over her chest and her hair was still lank and listless. *Fuck*, she reprimanded her reflection, *you look like a worn-out old whore.*

Grabbing her bag and coat, she went out to her car, but when she turned the key in the ignition, nothing happened. She tried again and again. 'What the fuck? You fucking, fucky car,' she cursed loudly, banging on the steering wheel in frustration. She didn't have time for this; she'd have to just leave it and get the bus in. If she was lucky, she could just make it, although the bus journey was at least forty-five minutes and who knew how long she'd have to wait for one to turn up.

Slamming the driver's door, she walked round to the other side, leaned over the passenger seat and retrieved her anorak. The bus stop was just at the end of her road and, as she was walking toward it, she saw a bus pull up. There was a queue of four people, which gave her a little time, and she ran for it, making it just as the doors started to shut. She was gasping for breath as she bought her ticket.

Downstairs was full so she made her lurching way to the top deck and grabbed the nearest seat she could before she fell over, shutting her eyes in order to black out the mad world.

It was 10.20am by the time she arrived at the college. In the Student Services, she bumped into Diane, who was looking frazzled, her cheeks flushed with adrenaline.

'Beth! I thought you might not come. We didn't know where you were.'

'Sorry,' Beth mumbled. 'My car wouldn't start and then the bus was stuck in traffic.'

'Why didn't you call?' Diane shot back accusingly.

'I forgot, it was rushed, I was trying to get here as quickly as possible.' She didn't mention that she'd almost fallen asleep and missed her stop.

'I understand that, but you need to phone us, Beth, if you are going to be late. We've had to re-jig everything. Gemma is with Becky now because we wanted to pair her with someone who knew about the course. I put Lee with Tom. You can relieve him but it might be better not to disrupt the class until after break. You can sit in here and do his job.'

Lee worked in the office, answering the phone and emails and referring students to the correct support team. He had level 2 BSL though, and was sometimes called upon to work as a CSW in emergencies like this.

Beth sat down in his chair and noticed that his computer was logged on to his Facebook page and that he was halfway through writing a post about his breakfast. The phone wasn't ringing and Diane had stridden away somewhere, looking purposeful.

Beth opened a new tab on the internet browser and brought up her webmail account. She had two new messages. One was from Diane.

Where are you Beth? Why aren't you answering your phone? Are you alright?

Beth reached into her bag. Her phone was switched off; she'd forgotten it in the morning confusion. There were three missed calls from the office and one text message.

Please call the office

Beth sighed and rubbed her eyes, fiddling in her bag to find a packet of paracetamol. She took three, swigging them down with the cold tea left on the desk by Lee.

Her other email was from *nostrings*. *You have an admirer*, it told her. She clicked to open the message and followed the link to the site. She'd have to clear the browsing history later but she wasn't really sure how to do that. The message was from *Jason3*; he was 24.

Hiya, I fancy mature women like you, how about it?

Just then, Diane came back into the room, marching over toward Lee's desk, a pen behind her ear. Beth tried to close down the internet but got some sort of 'are you sure you want to' message. She had no time to read it and hastily switched off the computer monitor, leaving her staring at nothing.

'Photocopy these, will you?' said Diane, slamming the pile on the desk, 'I need them in fifteen minutes.'

As Beth headed for the copier, she saw Diane sit down at Lee's desk and switch the monitor back on. She felt utterly sick: it was all there for Diane to see. She was standing by the photocopier trying to breathe when Diane was suddenly upon her.

'Beth, what do you think you were doing?'

'I was just checking my email and then that popped up.'

'Come on, I wasn't born yesterday, it didn't just "pop up" did it, Beth?'

Beth shook her head and stared at the floor, willing it to fall away under her.

'Checking your personal email is inappropriate anyway but looking at dating sites in college is totally unacceptable.'

'I'm sorry,' she mumbled.

'It's a very busy morning and you are the cause of most of the problems: I can't have it. This is unprofessionalism at its utmost.' She paused and lowered her voice, 'I have already warned you and this is your final warning. If I hear so much as a squeak about you failing to fulfil your role then I will have to go to disciplinary, got it?'

Beth nodded, crumbling inside.

At break time, she headed for the canteen, hoping that coffee could do something to bolster her against this monstrous day. As soon as she walked through the door, she spotted Gemma and Lee sitting together laughing. She turned quickly so that her back was toward them and headed for the coffee machine, hoping they wouldn't see her.

'Beth!' she heard behind her. 'Hi! Thought you weren't coming in? Come and sit with us.'

Beth turned to Gemma and tried to smile, pointing at the coffee machine. She put her money in and pressed some buttons, adding extra sugar, trying to think how she could get out of sitting with them. Her only idea was to turn straight round and walk out of the canteen to drink the coffee in her car, but then she remembered that she had no car and panicked. She felt someone touch her sleeve. It was Lee.

'Hi, Beth, I need another.' He nodded toward the machine. 'You alright?'

'Hmm,' she nodded, 'I've been doing your job.'

'We swapped! Me and Gemma were just talking about it, I don't know how you do it, takes a lot of concentration and I missed loads.'

'Don't listen to him!' Gemma's voice chimed from behind where she'd been listening. 'I told him it doesn't matter. He did his best I'm sure and, as I always say, some signing is better than nothing for these kids.'

'Young people,' chided Lee.

'They ARE young yes, it's brilliant the deaf students can come to college,' Gemma carried on. 'It's so rewarding to help them learn.'

Beth glanced at Lee. Was he taken in by this shit from Gemma? Did he see that they weren't helping anyone to learn, just making sure that the deaf students could access the information to let them learn for themselves? Did he see how important it was to get them clear information, as close to what all students got as possible? She couldn't tell. Lee was nodding at Gemma as if she was the fount of all knowledge and wisdom.

Beth felt even more sick. All she could see was Paula stroking the air in front of her and mouthing *patronising, patronising*. She needed to get out.

'Sorry,' she managed, 'I need to go and talk to Diane.'

'No worries,' Lee said, 'talk soon.'

With that, Beth hurried to the entrance of the college, tipped her coffee on the ground and half–ran for the bus stop.

The timetable said the next bus was in twenty minutes. She perched on the narrow, sloping seat in the bus shelter just as her phone rang. It was Diane. Without preamble she rattled, 'Are you coming in, Beth? Break is over and Tom's waiting.'

'Sorry, Diane, I've just thrown up, I'm going to have to go home.' It was nearly true, her insides were churning and her head was buzzing.

'And you were going to let us know, weren't you?' Diane asked tersely.

'Yes, of course, I just threw up.'

'You said. You must ring me in the morning first thing to let me know if you'll be here tomorrow. Remember what I said about disciplinary, Beth?'

And with that, Diane hung up. Beth waved two fingers at her handset and pressed her eyelids tight together until it occurred to her to text Rick.

Car fucked, can you check it out? He'd know about these things: why hadn't she thought of him before?

Sure, came the reply, *about 6 after work?*

Chapter 15

Beth could feel someone stroking, tapping and shaking her arm. She stirred a little. 'Beth, come on!' her eyes opened and she stared blankly around her.

'Beth, it's me. Come back to us, love.'

She knew that voice.

'Come on, Beth, sit up a bit.'

She was slumped over the kitchen table and pulled herself up to see Rick standing next to her, holding a mug of water and trying to get her to drink. She took the mug he offered, sipped it, and then started gulping until water dripped down her shirt front. She handed the empty mug back to Rick.

'Thanks.' She wiped her mouth, and then reality hit.

'What are you doing, Rick?! Why are you in my kitchen?'

'You said you wanted your car fixing.'

'My car?'

'Fixing. You texted that it's fucked. But when I came round you weren't answering your door and you let me stand outside freezing my bollocks off. Eventually, I came round the back and your back door was unlocked and I saw you slumped here surrounded by bottles and this mess.' He indicated spilled red wine.

'I hope this wasn't important?' he said, peeling a wine–soaked sheet of paper from the kitchen surface.

'Oh Christ,' Beth groaned, 'can you still read it?'

'I can see "I'm s". What is it?'

Beth's head dropped to the table. 'Fuck, I was looking at Dan's note.'

'What, the one he left before he pissed off?'

'Yeah.'

'Why?'

'I don't know. Sometimes I do.' She shrugged, 'For clues, I guess'. She looked at him and smiled ruefully, holding up her hands.

'I know, don't bother telling me: I'm a fuck–up. What time is it anyway?'

'Just gone half past six.'

'Shit.'

'I'll get coffee and then you'll tell me what's really going on.'

As he went to make coffee, Beth went to the downstairs loo to piss and splash cold water on her face. Then they both went to sit side by side on the sofa in the lounge, dipping biscuits in their drinks. Beth put her head back and sighed deeply.

'In your own time,' he said coaxingly, glancing at her.

'It's all gone blank again, pretty sure I had a crap day at work.'

'Is that new?'

'I almost got sacked, that was it.' Even as she said it, she felt there had been something else.

Something when she'd got home? Something from before?

'You almost got sacked?'

'For being late, for... other stuff.' She couldn't be bothered to go into it.

Rick was clearing up dirty dishes from around his feet when it came to her.

Please, Daddy?

'Oh fuck.'

'What is it?'

'I fuck everything up.'

'How's that?'

'Just everything, it doesn't matter.'

Beth burst into tears.

Rick put his arm round her. 'Come on, it'll be okay. I'm here,' he said lamely.

'I'm this close to losing my job, I lost Dan, I lost my dad, I lost…'

'No, Beth, none of that was your fault, what happened with your mum was not your fault, can't you see?'

'But if I'd only bothered to go with her I could have…'

'What? You could have what? Nothing, Beth.' He rubbed his eyes, 'Beth, after your mum, you pulled yourself back, and after Dan fucked off, you pulled yourself back for a long time. You made a career move, you got your life on the track you want. Why are you going back to square one? I can't help you, I'm not into this emotional shit. Have you seen your counsellor? Your doctor? There are drugs that…'

All of a sudden, Beth turned her head to face him: they were so close that their noses bumped together, and she tilted her head and kissed his mouth hard, forcing his lips apart. She felt his cock hardening against her thigh but he pushed her away gently.

'Don't do this, Beth, not now.'

Beth was crying. 'I'm sorry, so sorry, not even you want me.'

'Fuck off, "not even me".' He grabbed her arms and pinned them to her sides, shaking her slightly until she returned his smile. 'Beth, listen: You. Are. Special.'

'Special!' she scoffed.

'Yes, special. I admire you, you need help right now, that's all. See your doctor, see your therapist, let them get the Beth I know back. I can't be the one to get you back.'

Beth was silent. Rick seemed at a loss.

'Did you need me to look at your car?'

Beth almost laughed. Only Rick could think about her car at this moment. She straightened up.

'Yes, my car's fucked,' she said wiping her eyes. 'It won't start. Get it working, will you?'

'Rick to the rescue,' he cried, playing an imaginary trumpet and marching out humming a cavalry charge.

Chapter 16

Sam, 2010

Sam was drinking his tea with his new PA, Sarah, who asked how he'd got on with the process of getting support.

'Oh, it was tricky at first. I had no clue where to go, but then I found a great social worker who ran through all the options with me.'

'Yeah, it usually takes a while, with all the assessments of need and support plans, but in the end it's life–changing for people who are finding things hard. The last person I worked with…'

'Stop right there.'

'What, I'm not breaking confidentiality or anything.'

'No. No, it's not that, I just wanted to thank you for saying "people" and "person" instead of "patient", "client" or "sufferer".'

'Oh, ha ha, yes, she hated all that too, so I deleted it all from my vocabulary. Anyway, I always thought that talking about "my clients" would make me sound like some sort of sex worker.'

Sam laughed. 'I knew I was going to like you. Do you know what, it's going to be great to be supported by someone on my wavelength. Feels like I can be me again.'

He thought back to the time he'd used Home Care after he'd broken his arm.

'Have you ever been to the MS centre?'

'No, my doctor said I should back when I was first diagnosed but I never fancied it.'

'Why not?'

'I just had visions of dull, ill people sitting round playing bingo and watching daytime TV.'

'Now who's stereotyping?'

'Guilty.'

'You really should go, I'll take you. There are a few your age and many lovely people. I used to go with my last "client" before she went to a full–time care home.'

She grinned and Sam laughed. 'Take me to your brothel; when's a good time?'

'Wednesday afternoons are good, the social club's open house – not just for people with MS.'

'Let's go tomorrow then.'

The MS centre had quite an impressive new building and wasn't how Sam had imagined it at all. The social club was held in the bar area. The difference to a normal pub was that a lot of it was adapted for wheelchair users; there was a lowered section of the bar and even a lowered pool table.

Sarah knew her way around and led him to a table where a man of about his age was talking to an older woman in an electric wheelchair.

'Frida and Danny, this is Sam.'

They all greeted each other and asked after the person Sarah had worked with previously.

Danny wheeled himself to the bar to get some coffees and Frida asked Sam if he had MS.

'I do yes, have you?

'Yes, it's hitting me harder now, not even allowed to get up out of this thing.' She patted her chair just as another woman walked over and was introduced as her PA.

'Are you working, Sam?'

'Not any more; work kept finding less and less taxing things for me to do but, in the end, I couldn't even manage them.'

They talked about his job as a firefighter and Frida's previous job as a lawyer. She was doing some kind of MA with the Open University now. God knows how she managed that with her muscle wastage and failing eyesight.

Danny had by then returned with the coffee. It looked, to Sam, as if Danny's condition was the result of a stroke, since his speech was slurred and his movement reduced. It was fascinating and heartening for Sam to see the myriad disabilities that seemed to befall people and how well they appeared to be dealing with them.

In the course of the afternoon, they were joined by a girl called

Lisa, who had what sounded to Sam like 'Earl's Dance Syndrome'. She called it EDS so Sam did too; it was to do with her joints. As they were sitting round, listening to tales of Frida trying to park her wheelchair–adapted van in too-small disabled spaces, they were joined by another man with MS. He was deaf and had a PA with him who signed.

Sam spent the rest of the time transfixed by the signing. He'd never met a deaf person before. It turned out that the man's name was Gary and he taught Sam to fingerspell his own name.

Gary prodded his jaw with his right index finger.

'Easy,' voiced his PA.

Sam copied him; he would remember that sign.

'How do I sign "hard"?'

Gary lip-read that and prodded his right thumb tip into his left palm.

MS hard, Sam signed.

Gary shook his head,*no*, and prodded his jaw as he rolled his eyes, *no, easy.*

They laughed.

'Pfft, how do you sign "stupid"?'

Gary turned to his PA, who signed knocking on his head with his fist.

Sam pointed at Gary and signed – *stupid.*

He wished he could sign more; he thought everyone should sign. As if reading his thoughts, Gary said, 'You should do level one BSL, you're a natural.'

Sam struggled at first to hear Gary's speech, then got it and gave Gary the thumbs up. 'Where?' he asked.

Gary started signing to his PA, who got a business card from his wallet and said: 'I know this woman teaches BSL, she has Usher and lives near here.'

Sam wasn't sure what 'Usher' was but he took the card anyway.

He'd definitely follow this up. He felt like these people would help him to start something positive in adapting to his new life with MS.

Chapter 17

Beth, sitting behind the wheel of her car, turned the ignition. The engine purred into life, just as it had last night after Rick had rescued it. She had no idea what he'd done and, if he'd told her, she could neither remember nor care. It was working, that was the main thing. Sitting in her work 'uniform', with her sandwiches made and the clock showing that she was reassuringly early, she found that she just couldn't face pulling out. She could already feel her heart accelerating and her head beginning to throb so she turned the engine off and sat staring out in front of her. She leaned over, got her mobile out of her bag and dialled the college. After six rings, a breathless Lee picked up.

'Hello?'

'Aren't you supposed to name the college and ask how you can help?'

'I am, yes, sorry, I just got in and was literally walking through the office door when…'

'It's okay, Lee.'

'Am I talking to Beth?'

'Yes, it's Beth here.'

'Are you alright, Beth?'

'I'm not going to make it today. Probably not this week, hopefully Monday.' Her words came out in rush as she tried in vain to slow them down.

'I expect you'll need a note from your doctor.'

'Right, okay, I'll get one sorted out,' she grimaced, rubbing the bridge of her nose while trying to sound nonchalant, if a bit fluey.

'Alright, Beth, I'll talk to Diane. Quite like signing for Tom now rather than sitting here all day, to be honest. I'm improving.'

'Okay then, see you.'

Just before she ended the call, she heard Lee say, 'Are you sure you're okay, Beth?' but she didn't reply, wanting simply to get off the phone.

Perhaps she'd been curt with him, rude even, but, quite frankly, she couldn't care less.

She felt lighter after making the decision not to work this week. She had four days to herself before she needed to get Paula to her weekend of riding. Today felt like it was going to be one of her better days but she knew that trying to go to college, being taken for granted and hearing Gemma's wheedling-whining little voice would put an end to that. She needed space; she was going to conquer this. She hated feeling so low; she knew she was depressed. It was a good sign that she knew and could stand back to acknowledge it. Rick was right: only she could help herself.

She scrolled through her handset for her doctor's surgery and found the number and dialled it. She was in luck: thanks to a cancellation, she could see a doctor at ten that morning. Even better, it was with a woman. She had ten minutes before she'd need to set off so she texted Paula, enjoying feeling productive.

Hi Paula, I'm not working on Friday now so we could leave a bit earlier to avoid the traffic if that's ok with you?

She found the stables they were going to, typed the address into her satnav, and then switched on her car again to head for Riverside surgery, feeling rather more in control.

'What can I do for you today, Beth?' Dr Tina Hawes asked earnestly, her curly chestnut hair tied back loosely at the nape of her neck.

'I, erm, I can't work this week and I need to get a doctor's note.' Beth suddenly felt awkward in front of this bouncy-looking, fresh-faced woman.

'Right, well, I'll need to know what I can help you with, medically. Obviously I can't just issue notes without a valid reason, Beth.' She gave a small laugh. 'What's the problem? I see from your notes that we haven't seen you for some time, the last would be what…?', she glanced at her computer screen, '… 2006? You had a course of citalopram because you were struggling with your mental health. You stopped taking them after…' she glanced at the screen again '… about a year. What happened? Did they help you?'

She was looking Beth in the eye and smiling warmly. Beth felt herself relaxing. Tina wasn't being brusque and dismissive like some doctors.

'Yes, they did help, they made me very anxious at first, I almost stopped taking them because I felt wired, the slightest thing made me panic...'

Tina nodded sagely.

'... but I'd been warned that might happen and those feelings passed. Then I got to feeling more stable. I did feel a bit numb.' She paused.

'Emotionally numb do you mean?' Tina coaxed.

'Yes, like not sad but never happy either. I just wanted to sleep.'

'Yes, right, but they helped? You got your head back on track?'

'Yes, they stabilised me. I had a bit of counselling too but not much. I had more of that after... well, some time ago.'

'Yes, right, I can see that. She was reading Beth's back notes now and Beth wondered what they said about her, about what happened on her 16th birthday.

Tina Hawes turned back to Beth.

'So how are you now, Beth?'

'I'm struggling again,' Beth heard herself saying, her voice catching as she borrowed Tina Hawes's word.

'Right,' Tina touched Beth's knee, 'then you have come to the right place.' Tina smiled.

Beth nodded and Tina spoke again.

'Are you feeling very low, Beth? On a scale of one to ten where one is not low and ten is desperately low, where would you put yourself?'

'It depends on a lot of things; it changes.'

'On a good day?'

'Four.'

'And a bad day?'

'Seven or eight.'

'Okay, thanks, Beth, and do you ever think about harming or have you ever harmed yourself?'

'Erm... yes and no.'

'Sorry, two questions there.' Tina pulled her chair closer: 'Have you ever thought about harming yourself, Beth?'

'Yes.' Beth's voice dropped.

'And have you ever actually harmed yourself?'

'No.' She was whispering now.

'Okay, Beth, try not to worry. Mental health and depression is a part of life, but it should be seen as a treatable illness.'

Beth remained silent and Dr Hawes went on, 'I can give you some new pills to help stabilise your mood; these ones are called fluoxetine. You've probably heard of them as Prozac?'

Beth nodded, although she doubted the question needed an answer.

'You will probably notice a decrease in your sex drive for a while.'

Thank God, thought Beth absently, but her smile was an effort.

'Do you have any other questions?'

'Can I drink with them?' Beth thought of her wine: she could stop by Tesco on her way home.

'Yes, you can still drink some alcohol but I'd err on the side of caution. A small glass of wine now and then won't hurt.'

Beth wondered if she could possibly do that.

'Look, Beth, I don't like to just prescribe pills and send patients away.'

'That puts you in a group of about one,' Beth said sardonically and caught a glimpse of a smile on Tina's lips.

'People are realising now that there is a lot more to healing than relying on medication. It's called holistic care, looking at the whole person. I can refer you for counselling or CBT, which many people find very helpful. You can also think about meditation, massage, Pilates or yoga. You need to be proactive, Beth. I know depression makes you feel the opposite but the pills will help. Just don't expect miracles from the pills alone...' She trailed off but Beth made no comment.

'Beth, you look tired, go home and rest. I'll write a sick note for your work, are you okay to come and pick that up tomorrow?'

'Yes, fine.'

Beth left the surgery feeling washed out but positive and proud of herself for going there. She'd dealt with a lot of shit before and could pull things round again.

Chapter 18

Beth's head felt unnaturally heavy and her eyes barely flickered open. She could hear voices but they sounded very far away and were saying things that made no sense:

'Sixteen... came in last night... mother and brother died... suffered hyperbolic shock... unconscious since arrival... only relative we can find is her dad and he's the man we just saw next door...'

She stirred and the voices stopped at once.

'Beth? Are you awake, lovey?'

She felt a hand on hers and strained her eyes open, only to be blinded by bright white light.

'Turn the lights out,' she heard someone say.

'Beth, love, come on, you're safe in hospital now.'

She opened her eyes again and saw a nurse crouching beside her bed: 'Here she is!'

Beth wondered who 'she' was.

'I bet you need a cup of tea, lovey, I'll be back in a minute.'

As the nurse left, Beth remembered her terrible dreams of car accidents involving her mum. Just at that thought, she started to panic, crying out and gasping for breath. The nurse ran back in.

'It's okay, Beth, it's okay, you're safe now. You had a terrible shock, here, put this back on and breathe.'

Beth felt a mask go over her mouth but pushed it off.

'I need my mum, where's my mum?'

The nurse crouched down beside her, 'Oh Beth, love, do you remember anything from last night?'

'I had a terrible dream.'

'What did you dream, love?'

'I dreamed there was a car crash and my mum died.' Her heart was racing again, she was fighting for breath.

The nurse squeezed her hand and breathed with her until she was calmer.

'Do you remember how you got here?'

Beth shook her head. 'Why am I here? Where's my mum?'

'I think I'd better find the doctor and she'll explain everything, Beth. Look, you just rest now and I'll get you that tea and then bring the doctor along to see you, okay? We'll get you some more pills to make you feel calmer too.'

Beth's eyes closed; she felt so tired.

Beth was in a fug: the nurse was stroking her hand again. The doctor had told her that it wasn't a dream and that Tom and her mum were both dead. She'd had more pills and now she felt nothing, just empty.

The doctor had also explained that her dad was in the room next door but when Beth had asked to see him, she was told that it might be a few days before she could as her dad was struggling.

'But I can help him,' she said, trying to pull herself up. The nurse pushed her back gently.

'You both need your rest,' she said. 'Your dad will be desperate to see you in a day or two, but right now he is asleep.'

Beth shut her eyes and soon heard lowered voices outside her door. 'He's violent, the doctor this morning thought it might be some kind of stroke but that's unconfirmed. People do very odd things after such a terrible shock.' Then the world went blank again.

Later that night, Beth was alone in her room; the lights had been switched off. She pushed back her covers and found she could sit up easily so swung her feet to the floor and tried standing. She felt woozy but was able to remain upright and took some tentative steps to her door.

Looking out through the small glass window, she saw that all was quiet; there were currently no nurses at the dimly lit nurses station. She eased open her door and padded along the corridor to the room adjoining hers. Checking through the window, she saw her dad asleep in his bed so she slipped in, crept toward him and curled up next to him on the bed.

'Dad?' she whispered, 'Dad? It's me, Beth, they won't let me see you.'

He didn't stir so she lay there with her head on his chest until a nurse came in and tried to pull her away gently.

'Beth, your dad needs his sleep. Let him sleep, love, come on.'

Just then, her dad woke up with a scream, and the nurse put a light on, pulling Beth back as her dad looked right at her.

'Get her away, get her AWAY from me!'

The nurse half–pulled Beth from the room, and as her dad continued to shout and rave, Beth felt herself convulsed by heart-wrenching sobs.

Back in her bed, the nurse held her. 'It's okay, Beth, it's okay, he doesn't know what he's saying yet, love. I know you need him, he'll be okay. In a few days he'll give you the biggest hug ever.'

Beth was shaking, numbed.

Chapter 19

Beth had managed not to drink anything last night, and she'd had a bath and watched a DVD in her dressing gown. Paula had texted in a panic around teatime, saying that she had a routine eye appointment but that Donna, who was going to take her, had had to go somewhere at the last minute. It was the last text that convinced Beth:

I immediately thought of you, Beth

If that was meant to butter her up, it worked. She'd agreed to go with Paula, who would give her cash in hand, since she was supposed to be incapacitated from work.

She woke feeling well, clearer-headed than most days, probably due to staying off the booze. She had decided not to start the pills until after the weekend because she remembered the initial anxiety caused by the last lot. She'd rather wait.

She couldn't say that she was excited by the idea of a second trip to the doctor's in two days, but it made a change taking somebody else, and she was interested to see how an appointment went with a deaf-blind patient.

The eye hospital had recently moved to its new building, which was bright and clean and white, and very airy. None of the expected hospital dreariness and stale antiseptic smell. With Paula on her arm, Beth checked the appointment letter and went to find clinic G.

They went to sit down to wait. It was bright, with unforgiving UV lighting, and Paula took a peaked cap from her bag in order to shield her eyes from the glare. Paula signed to her:

Before we go in, you should know that I don't have Usher.
You don't? Beth was taken aback.
No, I have other complications with my eyes.
So how come you said you have Usher?

89

Well, Paula paused a moment, *Usher is the most common cause of deaf-blindness, it just seemed easier. People will have heard of it. There was an Usher social group near me when I was a teen,* she continued, *and my social worker tried to get me in but they refused. They said it was for people affected by Usher only, despite deaf-blind people having very similar challenges on the whole.*

Right.

A bit silly. Anyway, when my social worker asked, they didn't know who I was so I went along later with my mum and we said I have Usher and I got in. I don't think it's a bad con.

Beth realised how little she knew about Paula and how much she didn't know about how Paula had dealt with things in the past.

'The doctor's ready to see you now,' the receptionist called over, breaking the silence that had fallen between them.

'Is the interpreter here?' Beth voiced at Paula's prompting.

'No one has checked in. What language are they interpreting into?'

Beth signed all this to Paula and they both laughed, hitting the sides of their heads with their fists to sign 'duh, stupid!'.

'A BSL interpreter. British Sign Language,' Beth added, in case the receptionist didn't know what BSL stood for.

'Oh right, yeah, I thought you were here to do that?'

Beth briefly explained the intricacies of interpreting, the importance of the patient getting full, clear and accurate information. She emphasised that she only had level three BSL to an interpreter's level six and was here as Paula's guide and PA only. It felt to her that she went over this same spiel again and again, and tried to temper her mounting frustration.

The receptionist picked up the phone to ring the agency and then reported: 'They haven't heard anything, the interpreter's phone is switched off.'

What?! signed Paula when Beth passed this on. *You'll have to do it, Beth, your signing is good.*

Oh, here we go, Beth thought, her mind reeling, 'Beth will do it'. What could she do? The only option was to go ahead with it: she could hardly leave Paula to go in by herself and not understand a word.

OK, she signed resignedly, *let's go.* Paula now took her arm and they walked to the windowless treatment room, where Paula sat in a padded black chair to the side of the consultant's desk and Beth pulled out a chair opposite.

'How are you, Paula?' the doctor asked in a soft, gentle voice.

Fine, thank you. Paula gave a thumbs up and Beth didn't bother voicing that, sure he'd understand.

'Any problems or changes with your vision?' So far so good, Beth thought. These were okay things to sign and voice, and the doctor was looking at Paula as he spoke and not directing his words to Beth: this was good.

No, same, the light still gets me.

'Okay, let me look at your eye.' He pulled out a machine on wheels and asked Paula to put her chin on the chin rest, turning off the main lights as he did so but continuing to speak.

'I'm just going to shine some lights in your left eye and get a better look at the cornea.' Beth tried to sign this information to Paula, who signed something back, but it was too dark to see her. Beth asked the doctor to put the main light back on while he explained to Paula and turn it off only when he started the examination. He did this willingly, but when he had the lights out again and after shining several bright lights into Paula's eyes, he asked her to look up.

Beth tried to sign this but Paula made a 'nnnn' sound so she asked the doctor to put the main lights back on again.

'Please tell Paula everything she will be asked to do before the light goes out. If not, it's too dark for her to see me signing.' She heard the exasperation in her voice as she put emphasis on *every-thing*.

Seeming not to notice, he calmly explained to Paula that, when he tapped her on the right arm, she should look right, and left when he tapped her on the left arm. He would tap her head for up and her knees for down. Paula was okay with that, although by now Beth was beginning to feel a bit unsettled.

The doctor put out the lights again and proceeded with the examination in silence until he said that he was going to put drops in Paula's eye in order to get contrast. Beth began to sign this but heard another, more aggressive 'nnnn' from Paula. Instead of asking the doctor, she reached for the light switch herself, feeling colour rising in her cheeks.

To her horror, Paula was crying, holding her hands over her eyes. Beth sat there awkwardly for a moment before she leaned forward to put her hand on Paula's knee.

Sorry, Paula signed, looking out from behind her hand, the light. *Bright/dark, bright/dark. Straining. No hat.*

Paula's signing was staccato, and she covered her eyes again. Beth looked at the doctor, who asked her what the problem was, and she told him that it was the light and that Paula needed a break.

'I can finish there,' he said, and started writing in Paula's notes.

The two got up and left, both looking rather more battle-worn than when they'd gone in. By the time that Beth had dropped Paula off and driven home, she felt completely drained. She had, however, realised two things: that she had so much more to learn about supporting deaf and deaf-blind people; and that that in itself was exactly what she wanted to do. She would ask Paula about doing her level 6 BSL and achieving a full interpreting qualification. The trip had also helped her to see beyond her own struggles.

Chapter 20

Sam, 2012

Sam's BSL course was coming to an end. He had enjoyed it immensely and loved being able to sign more with Gary at the centre. His teacher, Paula, had made it all a lot of fun and she was now running through the details for the students' final assessment the following week. They'd have to sign about work and he felt sad that he'd be signing about an ex-job. He'd gone from fire prevention to office dogsbody until even that had been too much for him. He seemed to be fighting this sad, frustrated anger all the time.

The classroom was part of an extension to Paula's house so, after class, her partner was able to walk in from the kitchen with a cake, as instructed by Paula's students. Sam was drawn back to the present just as his fellow learners pulled out party poppers and signed 'for she's a jolly good fellow', before giving Paula a present and thank-you card for getting them through the course. Paula clapped her hands and hugged them all in turn, offering drinks while someone cut the cake.

Sadly, Sam couldn't stay: Ollie was coming for the night. Despite asking, many times, Kim still wouldn't settle on a routine and seemed blind to the strain that it put on Sam. Of course he was excited to have Ollie, but it was very inconvenient.

Ollie and Kim were already waiting outside the house when he got back and Ollie had his football under his arm. Sam's heart sank: it was still warm, late afternoon, and Ollie would want to be out, running about in the garden. Sam could already feel his legs buckling. He'd had nothing but cake since mid-morning, and had to eat something nourishing.

'Dad!' Ollie ran to him oblivious, 'Can we play football?'

'Sure!' he said, letting Ollie pass him and turning to talk to Kim, but she was already on her way to the car.

'We have to sort out a regular time for Ollie to visit!' he shouted, as she shut the car door. This lack of fore-planning and the seeming randomness of Ollie's visits had been going on for years and he couldn't hack it much longer. He always felt under pressure to comply with Kim's whims, to say 'yes' each time, so that at least he could see Ollie.

'Are you hungry, Ols?' Sam asked.

'No, I just want to go outside.'

Sam let him out, feeling exhausted tears building, wanting with all his heart to play with his son. The tears were another thing he'd never had before the MS.

'I'll be with you in a minute, just going to get some food.'

As he opened the fridge to get some eggs, Sam re-read the mantra he had stuck on there. It wasn't a direct quote but it was his take on it:

You can't control the shit life throws at you but you can control how you deal with it.

He smiled, it always made him feel better. He could deal with this. He'd have his eggs and then go out and do his best. After all, there was no point dwelling on what he could no longer do.

As he was eating, he devised a new game called 'hit Dad's feet' where he could just sit in a chair and Ollie could see how many times in a row he could accurately hit dad's feet.

Ollie loved it. They played until it was time to get dinner ready, by which time Sam was getting very bored and was itching to get up and run. It was something, though; at least he could be a dad with his son.

They played cards after tea until Sam sent Ollie off to bed. He turned in himself not long after, unable to keep his eyes open.

In the morning, given Sam's slowness waking up, Ollie had promised to get himself up and ready for school. True to his word, Sam could hear cupboards banging in the kitchen. Despite his exhaustion, he got out of bed because he wanted to see Ollie before his mum picked him up.

'Morning, Dad,' Ollie greeted him, without looking up from his cornflakes. 'You were out of milk so I went to Mr Singh's and got some more,' he added proudly.

'Good work, Ols,' he said, ruffling the boy's unbrushed hair. 'You'd better get your things together, Mum will be here soon'

Ollie dutifully stood up and took his bowl to the sink.

'And brush your hair!'

'Aye aye, captain,' he saluted, turning to the door.

'Give your dad a hug before you go.' Ollie walked back over to Sam and hugged him. He'd got his mum's thick dark hair and large soulful eyes and he looked set to have his dad's height.

Now that Sam was officially disabled, he'd come to see beauty as an odd kind of disability. No one got it when he said that, but if you looked at disability in terms of an impairment creating barriers to accessing every day life then it kind of made sense. Barriers could be physical, which wasn't really applicable to beauty, but they were also attitudinal – how people reacted to you. He'd learned all this stuff from Frida, the lawyer at the MS centre.

He felt that possessing outstanding beauty affected the way everyone treated you and how they acted around you. It affected how they thought you'd be and what they expected from you. Often, it got you on an easy road to success: yes, he would admit that. But often, too, it made it difficult to interact with people without your looks being an issue. He'd had it with women blushing and blustering in his presence, gay men flirting, and straight men threatening to beat up his 'pretty-boy face'.

Kim got it, too, with most men seeming to be incapable of talking to her without wanting her. It was no wonder that she felt her looks were her only asset; that's what life had taught her. Beauty had become a kind of self-fulfilling prophecy for her. He just hoped that Ollie wasn't going to be too beautiful in ways that might make his life difficult.

When the doorbell rang, Sam went to the door and there she was: hair tied back in a ponytail, wearing skinny jeggings with a thick brown coat, and trying not to look like she'd made any effort in getting ready. He knew that she often took even longer than usual when trying to perfect this yummy mummy look. Getting the right balance between looking casual, sexy and cool took a lot of time.

'Ollie, you ready? Your mum's here!' he shouted back in the direction of Ollie's room. Thankfully, the boy appeared in seconds and ran to his mum, who kissed his forehead.

'Hi Ollie, your dad looked after you?'

'Yeah, we played "hit Dad's feet".'

'Cool,' she glanced at Sam with an unreadable expression on her beautiful face and didn't bother to ask for details. 'Thanks,' she managed, 'we have to go'.

'Any time.' Sam wanted desperately to talk to her, tell her he wanted to see Ollie more often, have him overnight on a regular basis. 'I'll call you.'

Every time Ollie left, he felt the hole in his chest growing just a bit more. He shut the door and collapsed against it. The constant battles with Kim, being allowed so little time with Ollie, facing muscle wastage and exhaustion: it all left him feeling totally emasculated.

Chapter 21

Beth, 1992

Coming back to school had been awful; no one had known what to say to her. The teachers all shook their heads in sympathy when they passed her in the corridors, putting a hand on her shoulder. Kate had taken it particularly hard because she had always been a little bit in love with Tom. Even then, she couldn't understand Beth's silences and refusal to ever talk about it.

Now though, one year on, everyone seemed to have forgotten that the accident had ever happened, but Beth was still locked in her shattered world. She still couldn't really talk to her friends and they were drifting away.

It was some surprise, then, when Kate brought her tray to Beth's table at lunch.

'Hiya, Beth.'

'Hmm,' she said without a smile.

'How're you doing?'

Beth just inclined her head and Kate got hold of her hand. 'I know we don't talk much now but it's because no one knows what to say. We were talking and hoped you'd come to the Scene with us tonight?'

No words would come out of Beth's mouth. She couldn't even think about that place any more. Her life outside school was taken up by sitting in her room at Anne and John's house or having sessions with the counsellor she had to go and see.

'I could come and do your hair, it's going to be a great night, they're having...', Kate babbled on but Beth was zoning out, '... we miss you, Beth. I miss you.'

Beth looked at her friend and swallowed, her food untouched.

'Thanks,' she managed, 'I can't tonight, my dad's coming round to Anne's.'

'Your dad is? How is he?'

'Yeah, getting a bit better. He's moved into a supervised flat.'

Kate blinked and Beth was aware that this was the most they'd talked for ages, apart from banalities.

'My mum thinks your dad had a stroke?' Kate made it a question and Beth sensed that she'd been waiting for the right moment to find out.

'No, doctors think now it was just shock, you know like shell shock we're doing in history or something.'

She dried up again; it was painful to talk about her dad. She would visit him once a week and he could tolerate her holding his hand as long as she didn't talk too much. Everyone assured her that he would get better in the end and she could see that he was, little by little.

Kate saw the shutters coming down again over Beth's face and said, 'Well, another time at the Scene though?'

'Hopefully,' Beth lied.

Some of the other girls came over then and Kate was soon locked in conversation. Beth was able to retreat into silence again, where she didn't have to think.

Anne and John were the third family she'd stayed with. Their house was pristine. Anne said she should have seen it when she'd had her kids running about. They were all grown and gone now and Beth was the only person who they were fostering at the moment.

She let herself in and Anne came out of the kitchen to greet her.

'Hi, Beth love, how was your day?'

'Okay,' Beth managed, already heading for the stairs.

'Your dad's coming in an hour,' Anne shouted up to her, 'I made a cake for us all.'

When the doorbell went again, Beth had changed out of her uniform. She hadn't seen her dad outside of his flat before and she felt nervous.

She could hear Anne showing him through to the lounge and saying that she'd go and put the kettle on for tea, then calling for her that her dad was here. Beth forced herself to go down.

Her dad was sitting in John's favourite armchair with his arms folded. He looked a little better: clean-shaven and smarter. Beth wondered fleetingly if he'd come to say that he was ready for them to move back home, though she wasn't at all sure what she would say if he did.

Instead, he took two sets of keys from his pocket and put them on the coffee table.

'Beth,' he said, the first time he'd uttered her name for a long while. Beth went forward and perched on the edge of the sofa.

'These keys,' he went on, holding up the first set, 'are for the old house.'

'The *old* house? Do you mean home?'

'The house we used to live in.'

'Right.'

'It's been sold.'

Her head flew up.

'No need to look like that. I sold it, I'm not going back there again.'

Beth's mouth went dry and her tongue knotted again.

'The house clearance people are coming in two weeks' time so if there is anything you want in there, you can go and get it.'

Beth's mind reeled. She had been back once with a social worker to pick up essentials: clothes, school stuff, a few CDs, but there was still so much in there that she wanted. On the other hand, she couldn't bear to go back to the house, not yet.

Before she could really think about it, her dad picked up the other set of keys.

'These are for your new house.'

'My new house?'

'Yes, I bought it in my name, obviously, but it's ready for you when you turn 18.'

'You bought me a house?'

'That's what I said.' He shrugged like it was a minor thing.

Just then, Anne came in with a tray of tea and slices of cake.

'I thought you'd probably need this.'

Beth looked at the tray in despair, unable to process anything her dad had said. She had a house, but what about money? What about university? A possible gap year? She didn't really want those things, but she might. How was she going to live by herself in a house?

Her dad was accepting the cup Anne held out to him, seemingly satisfied that business was over. Beth would have so many questions. Where would he go once he got well enough to live independently?

'Come on, Beth, we have to celebrate you becoming a propertied young lady.'

So Anne knew?

It was too much. Beth turned round and ran upstairs.

Chapter 22

Once she'd driven home, Beth remembered that her phone was switched off in her bag. After rummaging a little, she found the phone, pressed it on and found a message alert: it was a text from Rick.

Will be in the Miller's later, fancy a drink (or 3?) 7pm?

Beth's eyes were itchy with fatigue but it was only 3 o'clock. She could go home and shower, eat, and flop in front of some crap on telly for an hour at least. After that, a drink (or 3?) would probably be good. She also felt that there was some air between her and Rick that needed clearing.

She got to the pub on the dot of seven and looked round for Rick, catching John's eye in the process. He waved and pointed toward the far booths where Rick was already sitting. 'You're early,' she said and then glanced down at the table, 'what the hell is that?'

'I finished work so thought I might as well come straight here and this is officially called a Blue Vomit or something, I thought we should try something new. It's good for you, you know?'

Rick seemed flustered, and not his usual laid-back self. He was pouring Beth a glass of Blue Vomit and staring at the jug and glass in earnest concentration.

'I'd really prefer a wine, Rick.'

He looked up, disappointed. 'Try this first, it's lovely. It's not really called Blue Vomit, it's blue something or other. I asked John for a pint and he told me it was happy hour on cocktails and that I should try his Blue something or other because you will like it.'

'Me?! How did he know you were meeting me?'

'I don't know, probably because I only ever come in here when I'm meeting you.'

Beth accepted the glass he offered her.

'Cheers!' they said together and clinked glasses. She took a tentative sip, bracing herself, but, in fact, John was right: she liked it and took another gulp.

'It's nice, what's in it?'

'God knows. Blue stuff. Gin? Tequila maybe. I'll ask John next time I go to the bar.'

They sat in silence for a bit; something had changed between them.

Rick sighed. 'Look, Beth, about before,' he paused, 'you know, the snogging, the staying at yours…'

'Snogging? Are you 12?'

'Beth, come on.'

'Sorry.'

'Well, about all that…'

'Yeah, I know. We're mates, you're married.'

'We're mates and I'm married,' Rick echoed in agreement, looking relieved. There was another pause.

'And? But?' Beth prodded, sensing more, wanting to say more herself but not knowing exactly what.

'I like you, Beth, I mean, I really like you but…'

'We're mates and you're married?' Beth's tone was questioning.

'To be honest, Beth,' he said at last when she just carried on staring at him, 'I'm not sure what I want to say. I care about you and I don't want to mess you about. I want to apologise for trying it on with you.'

He looked so sheepish and unsure of himself that Beth was churning in embarrassment for him but tried to sound light.

'Rick, please, forget it, we're mates, I'm glad to have you as a mate,' she emphasised the last word, 'and anyway, I think you'll find that I was the one who tried it on with you.'

He nodded and then shook his head, smiling now. Beth nodded repeatedly and over-exaggeratedly and they both downed their glasses. 'Right then,' he said, pouring more, 'that's cleared that up. So what have you been up to since I last saw you, *mate*?'

Beth smiled slightly. She wasn't sure where to start or what to tell him but then she thought 'what the hell' and told him about the sort-of panic attack she'd had at work, how she'd been to her GP to get pills, taken the rest of the week off, and then spent most of today in hospital with Paula and seen her cry.

'Wow, Beth, you don't like routine much, do you?'

'I don't like my job much, I think you mean.'

'Is it the job that's upsetting you, or the date?'

She looked at him properly. He knew her better than many people did, if anyone else really knew at all. It might be the effects of two glasses of Blue Vomit but she felt totally at ease with Rick.

'Maybe both,' she admitted. 'I hate the job, I hate the attitude of patronising condescension to the deaf students, as if they should be grateful for the "help" they get from us, even when it's second or third rate. I want to be able to give them more support practically. The word is empowerment. I want to empower them.'

'Fuck, Beth, I'm only a salesman, I know words like bowl, cup and deal.'

'OK, suffice to say, the job pisses me off every day and then this week I can't take it.'

'You don't seem depressed.'

'Depressed people don't always seem depressed, Rick. They don't even always feel it, at least I don't. Not always. It can sweep over you and at the worst times, you just can't see out, you can't face anything.'

There was a pause. Rick looked nervous at the mention of depression.

'Beth,' he said eventually, pouring the last half–glass each of the blue stuff into their empty glasses, 'when your mum went…'

'Died, Rick.'

'Yeah, died, you've never really said what happened after. I mean, what happened to you? You were, what was it, 18?'

'16.'

'You were 16, I mean, your dad is a fruit-loop, how did he… how did you…?'

Beth told him what had happened with her dad's slow recovery and him buying her a house.

'So did your dad bugger off straight away?'

'To Spain, you mean?'

Rick nodded.

'No, he was a year or so in sheltered housing. It took him a while to get back to a semblance of normal in his head. When I was 18, though, I was an adult in his eyes so he set me up in my house and got on a plane. He'd done his bit and he was going.'

'So you were 18 with no family and a house to manage?'

'No family, no friends, no job, not many qualifications.' Beth squeezed her eyes, as if trying to lock the memories inside or, better still, block them from getting back in now that she'd got them out to Rick. 'But I did have a house at 18, not many people can say that. I shared all this with Dan, the counsellor knew, obviously, and the social worker who helped me but aside from them, no one really knows.'

'Wow, Beth, I'm honoured,' Rick said, grinning to try to lighten things. 'You are amazing, Beth.'

'Most people have shit in life, I just got mine early.'

'What did you do? You know... next?'

'The social worker helped me to get a job in the furniture department of Habitat and I worked there until a job came up with a company called Better Solutions UK selling hoists and bath chairs.'

'Really? Shite Solutions was your second–ever job?'

'Yep, second ever.'

'And then you met me.'

'And then I met you and we all lived happily ever after.' Beth smiled, feeling nicely cloudy-headed. 'So now you know and we can talk about football or anything you like as long as it's not me.'

'One more thing, Beth.'

'Go on then.'

'When did you last see your dad?'

'Not since I was 18.'

'You can't be serious?'

'We speak on the phone, he never asks to see me.'

'And do you ask to see him?'

'No.'

'What if you did?'

'I don't know that I want to, he's a shell of my dad, I can't relate to him.'

Beth couldn't face going into details with Rick but, truth was, she found it so hard to shake the images of her dad pushing her away when she went to hug him or, worse, screaming at her in the hospital.

'But he must have some social flair,' Rick went on, 'why else would that woman have a baby with him?'

'Vivien? I don't know, I've never been able to work that out.'

'Would you like to find out?'

'I guess I would,' she surprised herself by saying. 'He hurt me more than I've told you after the accident but rationally I know he wasn't being himself.'

'Then why don't you go and see him now? If you don't want to ask then just turn up at their house.'

'Maybe I should, maybe that's a great idea.' She paused before saying, 'I love you, Rick,' and walked round the table to give him a drunken hug.

Beth woke before it had started to get light, and felt the familiar desperate thirst and dull, aching head. Putting on her bedside light, she reached for her water and became aware of movement beside her.

'God, Beth, too bright!' She jumped, looking round and yelping, almost bumping heads with Rick who was sitting up, rubbing his eyes.

'Oh my God, Rick!'

'Morning, mate,' he grinned, in his usual phlegmatic way, 'well, oops, I guess we had too much to drink again.'

Beth pulled the duvet up round her naked shoulders.

'You do remember, don't you?' she asked, because she didn't, and hoped to bluff her way to pretending she did. This was another level to finding Rick on her sofa.

'Course I do, I walked you home and then you invited me in and then...'

'Yeah,' Beth cut him off, 'that's okay I remember now, bit of a blur though, but... shit, Rick!' She put her face in her hands.

'Not to worry.'

'Not to worry?!'

'It wasn't my plan, you know?'

'What *was* your plan?'

'No plan, I was going to apologise for before, clear things up between us.'

'Well, I guess that's one way of doing it.'

'I guess so.'

They stopped talking and Rick fell back on the pillows and let out a huge sigh. 'Sorry, Beth, I blame the Blue Vomit.' Then he snorted some sort of snore and turned on his side away from her.

There was no way she could get back to sleep, so she switched off the lamp and crept out the room. She had to stop doing this – she didn't know where it would take her. She was friends with Claire, for Christ's sake. She was more Rick's friend but she did meet Claire for the occasional coffee too. Would they tell Claire? Could she ever look Claire in the eyes again?

She lifted the laptop from next to her on the sofa and put it on her knees. Switching it on, she logged into *nostrings*. She had two messages in her inbox but forced herself not to read them as she tried to find out how to leave the site. They didn't signpost that information but, after searching a while, she eventually found it in the help section and followed the instructions to remove her profile.

Are you sure you want to remove your profile and discontinue?

Yes

We would hate to lose you, would you stay with us with one month's free membership?

No thanks delete profile

Finally, they let her go.

Your profile has been removed. She closed the laptop down and sat back in her seat, resting her head on the cushions. No more *nostrings*, no more Blue Vomit. She closed her eyes, slightly pleased with her resolve. No more random sex? No more wine? She didn't answer her own questions.

When Rick eventually came downstairs, he was fully dressed and on the phone. Beth could only hear his end of the conversation:

'I *did!*', there was a pause, 'I was worried about her,' and another pause as Rick listened and shook his head, 'no, right, sorry.' There was some more talking, then he said, 'I love you' as he took the phone from his ear.

'She hung up. I'm not flavour of the month.'

'Was that Claire?'

'Course it was Claire.'

She remembered the 'I love you' comment. 'Yeah, course it was Claire. What have you told her?' she tried to sound calm.

'That we met for a drink, you got pissed and I had to bring you home and slept on your sofa again. My mate once said that the best lies are the ones nearest the truth.'

Beth didn't like how that version made her look but it was better than being someone who shagged a mate's husband, someone to whom she wasn't even attracted when sober, and then couldn't remember any of it.

'Well, it's done, it happened, water under the bridge.' Beth didn't feel any of that even as she spoke.

'Thanks, mate, you're right. It was just one of them things.'

Beth had a long shower after Rick left and then stood before her long mirror. Her boobs sagged down to her waist, like heavy sacks of water. 'Waist' was an optimistic term: it didn't really exist, there was barely any inward curve. Turning sideways to the mirror, she saw rolls of fatty flesh on her lower back, her stomach hung down slightly in a lumpy mass. She rubbed her face with her hands and watched her reflection copying the gesture. Again, seeing the bags under bloodshot, washed-out grey eyes. Holding her wet lanky hair up behind her head, she scrutinised the jowls hanging round her face.

The Beth in the mirror put her hand between her legs and moved it in small, gentle, massaging circles but the Beth looking at her felt nothing. She wanted to feel something, anything. There was no arousal so she pinched herself and felt pain. She carried on pinching, pulling, tugging at herself. The pain felt soothing; she felt a rush of adrenaline, a release of tension.

Anger flared up, and she felt suddenly full of rage: angry at Dan, angry at Rick, angry at *Rockman* and *Billybear* and *nostrings*, angry at her dad, her mum, Tom, angry at Gemma, Diane, the staff at the college. Angry at everything that was conspiring to ruin her life. Angry at her fucking fickle swinging emotions.

Chapter 23

Sam was up and doing his yoga and deep breathing by nine. He felt his mind clearing in readiness for the day. Karma-wise, he was in a pretty good place today. *Every day is a new day* was another of his mantras.

When Sarah arrived, he was stretched, fed and ready, and they went out for a coffee.

'You're looking better every day,' she said spooning the froth from her cappuccino.

'I know, I'm so relieved to be feeling strong enough for the weekend. These last few months have been hell.'

'How's the nerve pain?'

'Under control and at last I don't feel drowsy from the pills.'

The café was filling up and they had to raise their voices slightly to be heard.

'Anything I can help you with today after coffee? Do you need help packing?'

'No, not really, it's just nice to be out of the flat. You can push me round the park later. I can't be arsed to wheel myself and you have to do *some* work even if it is your official last day.'

'Officially it is my last, thank God!' she joked. 'Have you got someone else yet?'

'No, not yet, I need to advertise harder. Social services have offered me temporary home care and I will have to suffer that until I get someone.'

'I gave you loads of time to replace me!'

'I know, I just haven't motivated myself.'

'I'm irreplaceable, that's all.'

'In your dreams,' he said, throwing his sugar sachet at her, 'anyway, you've only officially left but not actually. We have the weekend to play first and I have to tell you where we're going so that you pack the right stuff.'

'You certainly do, you've been very cagey ever since you told me to keep this weekend free.'

'Yes, well, I wanted it to be a surprise.'

Sam got an envelope from the bag on the back of his wheelchair. 'Well, it's not an entirely selfless gift as I wanted to go myself and would have needed you to take me.' He pulled the letter out of the envelope, 'but I wanted to thank you for sticking with me so long. I feel very lucky to have had such a lovely PA.'

'Aww, it's been a pleasure.'

'Good luck with the marriage and the move.'

'Thank you so much.' She got up to hug him, 'Come on then, what is it?'

He handed her the booking confirmation letter from Becher's farm equestrian centre.

'Becher's we went to before?!'

'Yes, the same place.'

'Oh that's fantastic! I absolutely loved it there! I can't be sure I'll fit in my jodhpurs any more though!' She got up to hug him again and kissed him on the cheek this time too.

'It's for us both before I lose you to another man.'

Sarah laughed.

'It's so brilliant, Sam!' and then it occurred to her to ask, 'What's Ollie doing this weekend?'

'Kim's having him, I'll miss him, but then I always do. I seem to miss him between seeing him even more now he comes every week.'

'That's understandable. I'm glad you got it sorted with Kim, though.'

'Me too, although I think she has come to like her child-free Saturday afternoons with Ernesto-Enrico. I heard they nearly always have a weekend away on his monthly overnight with me.'

'You heard?'

'Yes, from Ollie. He makes a better informer spy now he's 10.'

'You nosy git!'

'Curious, that's all.' Sam held up his hands in surrender, 'I need to know what's happening in my boy's life.'

'Fair enough. It's all worked out pretty well, I suppose.'

'Yeah, I guess it has.' Sam recognised the apparent absurdity of the statement. The odd thing was, though, that he did feel his MS had led him down paths that were helping him to be his true self.

They got to the park and there was some sort of kids' cycle race going on, so they had to weave their way through careering bikes and out of the path of the puffing parents who were trying to keep up with them. Eventually they found a path that wasn't part of the race route. It was flanked by trees that were shedding their leaves, and Sarah had trouble getting Sam's chair through them.

Sam spoke into the air: it was weird having the person you were speaking to walking behind you.

'Have you got a date for the wedding yet?'

'Yes, we have!' Sarah's speech was full of exclamation marks. 'It's going to be 1st March next year.'

'Wow, that's pretty soon.'

'I know! Don't tell anyone but I just found out that I'm pregnant! We want to do it before I start getting much of a baby bump.'

'Wow!' Sam said again, thinking back to Ollie as a baby.

'We're not making it official yet so I try not to talk too much until I can be officially excited. To change the subject, Sam, what about you?'

'I'm not pregnant.'

'Idiot! What about your love life?'

'I've given up, don't like all the liars on the internet so I'm just waiting for Miss Perfect. Maybe I'm past it.'

'You're definitely not past it, Sam, you're one of the most amazing people I know.'

'Aww.'

'So describe Miss Perfect.'

'A realist, resourceful, open-minded, down–to-earth, thoughtful, caring... stuff like that.'

'That's just like you, most men would have started with "tall, leggy blonde".'

'I don't fancy myself.'

'Are you sure?'

'Watch it!'

'Look, give me a few weeks and I will find this woman.'

'Right, I'll leave it to you then.'

'I'll also look around for a new PA for you. I think I know some-one who might be interested.'

'That would be very cool.' Sam wondered how he was going to manage without her.

When Sarah dropped him home, he had all afternoon free. Luck-ily, he'd already started packing so he could get some rest in prepa-ration for going away.

After lunch, he got out his knitting, wondering what on earth his mates at the MS centre would say if they knew, never mind Mr Crosby, his erstwhile boss, and all the guys at the station. Not that he really cared. Knitting suited him; he loved being occupied and making things, and he found it quite meditative. Despite his clumsy hands, so far, he'd managed to make a pretty decent hat and his ulti-mate aim was a wearable jumper.

He thought how peaceful the day had been. As things were cur-rently, it had been the best kind of day he could hope for, and he mused at how long it had taken him to adapt to that fact. *Every day is a new day*, he repeated to himself.

Chapter 24

Beth, Friday

Paula stood in the doorway smiling and then turned to heave a massive, hard-shell suitcase down the step out front as she shut and locked everything. Beth got out of the car and went up to her so that Paula could see. They had to jig around a bit in order to get the sun behind Paula rather than silhouetting Beth in a dazzling halo.

Morning, Paula, is that all you're bringing? Beth teased.

Paula didn't get the intended sarcasm and answered straight:

Yes, that's all. I managed to get everything in one case because I packed my smaller shoes and am wearing these.

She pointed to her boots. They were a good pair of leather riding boots, not the cheap rubber kind. Beth hadn't got any at all and would have to borrow some. The centre website said they had boots in all sizes. She'd be borrowing a hat, too, but had packed two pairs of cord trousers, which they said would be fine for riding in: jeans were a big no-no.

She'd also put a box of six wine bottles in the boot of the car: just in case, she told herself.

Paula was already climbing into the front passenger seat so Beth hauled the enormous case down to the car and slid it across the back seat.

Who's got Barney? she asked Paula, slamming her door closed.

My mum and dad, he's staying with them all weekend.

Beth gave the thumbs up and started the car, keen to get on with the journey. She could get herself as far as the motorway turn-off and then had her satnav at the ready. She had the radio tuned to Classic

113

FM and was listening to a Haydn violin concerto, aware that Paula had only her thoughts to entertain her.

When they'd turned off the motorway, the countryside got more and more beautiful. Beth lowered her window and let in a blast of freezing air, breathing in the country smells. The monotone voice of the satnav told her that they'd 'arrived at their destination'. She looked around and could see nothing but fields, dry-stone walls and sheep. She tapped Paula and signed:

Is it near here?

Paula shook her head because she couldn't see enough to know where they were. Beth felt briefly panicked but drove slowly round the corner and saw a field of horses, then noticed a farmhouse in a distant field. That must be it. A few seconds later, there was a track bearing a big sign, hand-painted in red paint, which had dripped down the hardwood.

Becher's farm, Equestrian Centre it boasted, although Equestrian was spelled 'Equestan'.

She followed the sign to the disabled car park and pulled into the nearest available space, turning to Paula who punched the air and signed *well done,* feeling around for her door handle. There was a car pulled up a couple of spaces away and a man in a wheelchair was disappearing into the house. The woman, who looked late twenties, said hello as she locked the car and dragged two small cases in the direction the man had gone.

Do you fancy walking round outside a bit to stretch our legs?
Beth didn't add, *and to avoid any awkward meetings at reception.*

Yes, I'd love to go and see if any of the horses are in the stables.

Beth was relieved as they set off round the back, with Paula taking her arm. They bumped into a girl of about 16 who was carrying a bucket. She smiled and went on her way, setting it down in front of a stable where a horse looked out over the door.

Beth knew nothing about horses and thought that it looked like an old-fashioned carthorse, with its long shaggy mane and black–and–white–patched skin.

> *That's JR*, Paula signed, *walking toward the horse, you might ride him tomorrow. He's like an armchair to ride, very good for beginners, never jumps in fright.*

She reached out her hand and stroked JR's face, kissing his nose. Beth stood back and watched until Paula turned to her and beckoned.

> *Come and say hello. Come on!*

The girl with the bucket was still standing there, letting Paula stroke the horse. She handed Beth something that looked like the marrow-bone biscuit that dogs eat. Beth looked down at it warily.

'For JR.' It was obviously clear to the girl that Beth was clueless with horses. 'Hold your hand flat like this,' she held her hand out, 'and put the pony nut on your palm for JR to nibble off.'

Beth did as instructed and held out her hand. JR immediately stretched out his head and gobbled up the food. Paula looked delighted and gave him a hug.

> *Are there any more horses around?* She signed.

Beth couldn't see any and asked the girl. 'No, they're in the field or Alice is using them for a lesson. JR's having a day off today.' The girl reached out and scratched his ears affectionately.

They went straight to reception, which was empty save for a man behind a table. As soon as he saw Paula approaching he signed,

> *Name – me J-O-E.*

Paula clapped and laughed, giving him the thumbs up.

> *Name – me what?* she asked.

Joe glanced at Beth and asked her how 'P' was fingerspelled; she showed him, he nodded and managed the rest: *P-A-U-L-A.*

Paula clapped again and signed well done.

Name – her B-E-T-H.

Joe took in air, shaking his head slightly and looking down at his papers.

'Beth?'

'Yeah.'

'Sign that again,' he asked Paula.

B-E-T-H.

He got it this time and copied her, smiling. 'Welcome to Becher's,' he said to Beth, 'any problems, come to me. You two are in room number four with a view of the stables. Tea and coffee are available in the kitchen at any time. Alice made a fruit cake this morning and it's on the table, just help yourselves. Dinner will be at six, there are only three disabled guests and so you should all meet before then. Sam and Sarah are here already, they live not far from you.'

They located the room and Beth went to fetch the cases. When she got back, Paula was sitting on the bed she'd chosen. No asking. She wanted the one nearest to the door so she could get out to the loo more easily. Her poor balance would make her stumble in the dark so that was fair enough and it meant that Beth got the one under the window, which she preferred. Beth dumped the cases but was dying for a cup of tea before she unpacked so she told Paula she'd see her in the kitchen and went along the corridor.

The kitchen was big, with a long table and lots of pine cupboards. It felt friendly just looking at it. The man and the woman from the car park were sitting together at the end of the table and smiled at her as she came in.

'Would you like tea?' the woman asked, 'I just put the kettle on.'

Beth would have preferred to get her own and sit apart from them, or even in the lounge room, but they pushed out her chair and got her a mug, impelling her to join them.

The man spoke. He was good-looking, if a little strained-faced, and Beth felt immediately wary around him.

'I'm Sam.' He held out his hand and gave her a firm handshake. She thought he seemed cocky, sure of himself. 'This is Sarah.' He paused, probably expecting her to add her name, but she didn't.

'Well, hi anyway,' he carried on regardless, 'Have you been riding before?'

'No, I...'

'Oh, you'll love it, I started here. Only been twice before.'

Sarah sat down with a teapot.

'Sam's a natural.'

'Not sure about that, you're a pro!'

'Hardly.'

Beth let them banter between themselves, deciding that Sam was probably one of those people who was good at everything and that Sarah was probably in love with him. Then she noticed an engagement ring on Sarah's hand.

'Are you two engaged?' she blurted out.

'To each other? God, no!' Sam said pretending to strangle himself.

Sarah hit him and laughed. 'I'm getting married in five months but Sam here is single and on the market.'

'Shut up, Sarah!'

'It's true! Someone has to be your pimp.'

It was his turn to hit Sarah, laughingly. Beth envied their ease together and suddenly felt that urge to flee that she knew so well. She stood up and got a mug off the rack.

'Sorry,' she said, pouring some tea out of the pot and tipping in some milk, 'I'd better take this along to Paula.'

'Are you a PA?'

'Yes.' She didn't want to get into any conversations. 'Thanks for the tea, I'll see you later.' She picked up the mugs and hurried to the door as they said, 'see you' to her back.

Chapter 25

When he'd seen the woman in the kitchen, Sam had frowned. He remembered his group last time and how they'd bonded within five minutes of meeting but, this time, that didn't look likely to happen.

'She was quiet,' Sarah offered, reading his thoughts, 'probably shy.'

'Shy people often think that no one in the world understands them.'

'Where did that come from? Like you'd know.'

'A lot of people say that.'

Sarah smiled and got up to take the empty teapot to the sink and run water in it.

'More tea?' she asked Sam.

'Nah, two's enough. She might loosen up a bit over a game of cards later, it usually does the trick. Makes people communicate without the need to talk too much.'

'I saw her signing in the car park with the woman she supports.'

'Yeah?'

Sarah sat back down. 'I think the other woman is deaf-blind.'

'Oh right, my sign language teacher was deaf-blind, she had Usher. Funny if it's her!'

'I'm sure there's more than one deaf-blind woman in the country.' Sarah was picking cake crumbs off the table on a damp finger and putting them in her mouth.

'Yeah, you're right – but Joe did say they live near us...'

'True.'

Sam was still thinking about the woman they'd just met. 'Don't you think she looked sad? Her soul was sad.'

'Oh, now you're going all beardy-weirdy.'

'But do you agree? If not about her soul, her eyes, then?'

'Yeah, I know what you mean.'

'You know, when Alice teaches us to ride, she doesn't just teach

119

us how to sit on a horse and make it move, she teaches us how to communicate with it. Soul to soul.'

'Yeah, I know, we won't get past walking until the horse trusts us. I'd like to trot, maybe canter, but it feels like Alice will never let us. Are we still talking about that woman??'

'We can't progress from a walk until we're sitting just right and talking to the horse with our *souls*.'

He emphasised the word 'souls' and mimicked Alice's voice: 'My point is that Alice will get to that woman's soul, just you wait.'

'I wouldn't be surprised,' she looked at her hands but Sam didn't want to stop talking.

'You know what?' he didn't wait for Sarah to respond, 'I was thinking.'

'You?! Did it hurt?'

'Get stuffed! I was thinking how differently people react to stuff.'

'How do you mean?'

'Life seems to get on top of some people more than others.'

'What's your point now? Is it linked with that woman, Yoda?'

'It is senseless, life is,' Sam said in his best Yoda voice and Sarah laughed again.

Sam could see that she wasn't in the mood for a philosophical discussion about suffering and sadness so he left it for another day. Besides, it was probably better to wait and talk with someone who knew trauma first hand.

'Anyway, that woman looked sad.'

'You said that; are you infatuated with her?' she elbowed him in the ribs.

'No, no. Meeting her just got me thinking, that's all.' He sighed. 'Come on, let's get some fresh air before dinner.'

When they got back to the kitchen after seeing JR and going back to their rooms to freshen up, Joe was busy making salad and checking the lasagne in the oven. He was a big man with shoulder-length brown hair tied back in a ponytail. He was wearing an apron with 'CHEF' printed on the front in bold, black lettering.

'Hi, you two,' he grinned, 'are you settling in?'

'Yes, mate, thanks,' Sam said for both of them, 'we've just been out to see the horses.'

'Did you see Alice? She's looking forward to chatting with you again. She's coming to eat with us once she's settled the horses down.'

'Cool, no we didn't see her, but we saw JR and gave him some Polos.'

'That horse's teeth are gonna fall out before the end of the weekend.' They all laughed some more.

'Did Alice ever tell you the story behind JR's name?'

'No. Presumably whoever named him was a fan of '80s American soaps?'

'Ha ha, no, everyone thinks that.'

'It's not that?'

'No, you see, when we got him, JR had no name so we ran a little competition and the prize was to name him. The winners were a lovely couple called Jill and Ray. It's their initials, you see, "J" and "R",' Joe added, in case Sam and Sarah hadn't got it.

'Aww,' they both cooed, 'so cute.'

'Did you meet the other guests yet?' Joe asked once the general cooing was finished.

'Only one, the PA to the deaf lady.'

'Beth?'

'Possibly.'

'She's with Paula, deaf-blind woman. They both sign, I thought you might get on.'

'Did you say Paula?'

'Yes, you know her?'

'Does she have Usher?'

'I dunno, she is dead sensitive to light.'

'I think she taught me level one BSL. Do you know her name-sign?'

'Well, she has taught me fingerspelling, is that what you mean?'

'Not exactly, no. All deaf people and BSL users have a name-sign, it's like shorthand for someone's English name. Paula's name-sign is this,' he signed the two fists moving down his sides.

'What does it mean?' asked Joe, copying the gesture.

'Determined, stubborn, strong-willed, words like that.'

'Blimey! Have to watch her then!' Joe chuckled, 'What's yours?'

Sam signed spraying a hose.

'A gardener?'

Sam shook his head.

'A car-washer?'

He laughed, 'No! A fireman, I used to work as a fireman. Sorry, fire-*fighter*.'

'Wow, I didn't know that,' Joe looked impressed, 'and you, Sarah, what are you?'

'One of Sam's deaf friends gave me this name-sign.' She moved her bent index finger and slightly bent thumb in front of her mouth.

'Smiley?'

'Close, it means laugh.'

'Nice, I like that one, suits you. What am I?'

'You'll have to ask Paula that, a deaf person needs to name you in BSL.'

'Okay, I will ask her.' He took the lasagne out of the oven and checked it. 'It needs browning up a bit but I hope the others get here soon. I'm lucky this weekend, you all eat anything. I'm more than happy to cater for dietary needs but it's nice when there aren't any.'

'Can't wait for your lasagne.' Sam and Sarah sat down, looking to the door. 'Who else is here, apart from Beth and Paula?'

'A girl called Izzy. She's on her own tonight but her mum's coming tomorrow. Izzy was attacked by dogs and had half her face bitten off as far as I can see.' He waved his hand round his face.

'No shit! Is she not terrified of animals?'

'No, she rode horses as a kid. Her mum's hoping it'll give her some confidence back.'

'Let's hope so – is she coming to dinner?'

'I think so.'

Right on cue, a girl in her late teens or early twenties walked in with hair draped over her face.

'Hi,' she murmured without looking up as she sat down.

'Hi, you must be Izzy. I'm Sam and this is Sarah.'

He held out his hand but, like Beth, she didn't take it.

'Hi,' she repeated.

Sam tried hard not to stare at her face but it was impossible not to notice it. One cheek was pitted and covered by a massive scar, the tip of her nose was missing and her lips were a mess of scar tissue.

Luckily, at that minute Paula walked in followed by Beth, who led her to a seat at the end of the table and sat down next to her. Paula was busy concentrating and so Sam wheeled his chair to her side, waited until she was seated, and then touched her arm. Paula looked at him;

> *I know you*, she signed and Beth voiced, before Beth looked stunned when Sam signed back.
>
> *Name – me Sam.* (He used the sign '*fire-fighter*'). *Name – you Paula-strong-willed.*
>
> *Fireman S-A-M!* signed Paula in delight, as his face clicked into place in her mind. They hugged and then he turned to Beth.
>
> *Name – you what*, he signed.

He looked at Beth who looked happier than before, but still wary.

> *Name – me sorry?*
>
> *Name – you what?*
>
> *Sorry.*
>
> *Name – you what?* Sam was a little panicked: was he signing the question wrong? Beth looked very flustered too. He grinned to try to sooth the anxious atmosphere between them.
>
> *Name – me Sorry. B-E-T-H. Name-sign Sorry.*
>
> Then she voiced, 'I'm Beth, my name-sign is sorry.'

'Oh!' he voiced back, hitting his head, 'that's your name-sign?

'Yes.'

'Why?'

Because, Paula jumped in, *she's always saying sorry when she goes wrong or forgets.*

I don't like it, signed Sam.

Why? Beth and Paula asked.

'Because', Sam voiced, 'no one should apologise for being themselves.'

Beth looked at her feet as Sam looked at her. It looked to him like she wanted to say more. He should explain about how he knew Paula but there was movement behind her.

'Alice!' he shouted, wheeling past Beth and hugging a tiny woman with a mess of dry–looking curls. The woman pulled off her wellies and worn-looking wax jacket before she came into the room, hugged Paula and Sarah, and then turned to Beth.

'And you must be Beth? Welcome!' she gave Beth a hug too, which seemed to take her by surprise and wasn't returned, Sam noticed. 'And you', Alice continued, unperturbed, turning to the girl, 'must be Izzy. Lovely to meet you.' Izzy returned her hug half-heartedly.

Sam found it impossible not to like this woman: he'd half–forgotten the warmth and joy that came from her in waves. She bounced over to Joe and her five-foot-two frame was engulfed in his long, lumbering arms. The two of them seemed to be happiness personified and he felt a little lurch of longing.

Chapter 26

Beth, Friday and Saturday

Throughout dinner, fireman Sam mostly dominated conversation, engaging everyone. Sarah and now Izzy seemed most smitten. Beth focused on signing for Paula or voicing for the others when Paula and he were signing directly to each other. She didn't want to be the focus of his attention. If anyone spoke to her, she would answer in monosyllables, making it clear that her priority was including Paula in the conversation.

At one point, Joe asked Paula what his name-sign was and as soon as Beth relayed the question, Paula instantly signed two fingers together on each hand rising upwards from her head to outline a tall hat in the sign for *chef*. That name was very much to his approval. Alice then asked for one too and was christened 'Alice-horse', to which she clapped in delight. Fortunately, fireman Sam didn't mention Beth's name-sign again.

Izzy wanted one, too, so Paula signed *Izzy-face-torn* by clawing her hands in front of her face and moving them round. Everyone fell silent; even the non-signers could see what that meant. Beth had found the visual 'abruptness' of sign language difficult to accept at first but knew now that Paula wasn't trying to offend or mock, she was just describing what she saw, as was deaf culture. Izzy's face was her most distinguishing feature, so, to a deaf person, this name-sign was the obvious one to give her.

It was a very awkward moment and Izzy had a tear running down her cheek.

'Don't worry, Izzy, deaf people just describe what they see.' Fireman Sam soothed, voicing Beth's thoughts. 'The sign for China is this,' he said, pulling out the corners of his eyes slightly to narrow them. In international sign, the sign for woman is this,' and he made two exaggerated arches over his chest to indicate large boobs.

Izzy laughed a little bit then. Fireman Sam was good at saying the right thing.

I think Izzy like different sign, he managed to sign to Paula in his limited BSL vocabulary.

You can't choose your own, Paula signed adamantly, *a deaf person gives your name-sign to you.*

But, this weekend we name her different?

Why?

She feels very self-conscious about her face, Beth put in, *she's crying.*

Paula gasped and put her hands to her face. Beth understood that, by insisting on that name, she was sticking with the deaf culture she'd grown up with. Her apparent insensitivity also stemmed from the fact that she was deaf-blind, and her impaired senses were not allowing her to pick up the atmosphere or be aware of Izzy's anguish. As a PA, Beth felt it was her job to make sure she had a grasp of what was going on around her.

How about Izzy-long-hair? Beth suggested.

It was a compromise, but still somewhat described the girl: nobody really knew her personality or likes and dislikes yet. Sam nodded his approval and Paula assented too: Izzy-long-hair was christened.

Thank you, Sam signed to Beth when no one was looking.

To her horror, she felt herself blushing. She was sure he'd think it was because she was grateful for his approval but, inside, she was angry. Angry that he could be so patronising to Paula by thanking her, in the way that adults do to adults after a child has offended. It was patronising to herself by implying that she had any other motive than ensuring that Paula had full access to the world around her. Did he imagine that she'd been thinking about him and his feelings? He didn't have anything to do with it and the fact that he said his thanks to Beth proved to her that he had no sensitivity to living with deaf-blindness.

When dinner was finished and Joe had cleared away the apple pie, custard jug and empty bowls, Alice got up to announce that they would have a meeting now, and she disappeared out of the kitchen, returning with a folder. Inside there was a copy of everyone's application form and a bundle of papers that Alice handed around. The first was a sheet of 'housekeeping' issues: directions to the nearest pub, shop and doctor's surgery, hours of curfew, and house rules about cleaning up after yourself in the kitchen, the bathroom and so on.

The next was the itinerary: riding times, meal times. Alice read it out and said: 'All of you have ridden before except for Beth so, first thing in the morning, up to break time, all of you will be going to the field to catch your horses, bring them to the stables, groom them and tack them up. Our very able stable-hand Vicky will show you what to do. I will have a session with Beth and JR to introduce you to horsemanship.' She looked at Beth and grinned.

Beth felt both conspicuous and irritated. Alice seemed to forget that she was here as Paula's PA-communicator-guide first and foremost.

'But then Paula won't have support,' she said as she turned to Paula to sign her words.

'Don't worry, we'll help Paula,' Sam had chipped in immediately, 'I'll sign and Sarah can guide her.'

Beth's anger was rising once more. Sam only had level one; it was Gemma at the college all over again. But Alice was already telling Sam that that was a brilliant idea, even before Paula knew about it. When Beth explained to Paula, hoping she'd object, Paula was actually quite happy with the idea. Beth closed her eyes and counted to ten. If it was fine with Paula, she'd have to let it go.

At the earliest opportunity, Beth went to check that Paula would be okay to get back to the room later without her, and readied herself to go up alone. She was already thinking about the crate of wine in the car, which she didn't want to have to share. To her dismay, Paula wanted to come with her to the room so that she could Skype Donna before she went to bed.

She got the wine anyway, but, when she offered a plastic cup to Paula, mercifully she refused, focused as she was on swapping news with Donna. Beth worked her way through a bottle, looking out into the darkness before climbing into bed.

She had a fitful night, made worse by the fact that Paula turned out to be a very noisy sleeper. Being disturbed through the night by grunts and snores, Beth rarely entered deep sleep at all and woke feeling totally unrefreshed and remembering that she was now another year older.

Joe's hearty cooked breakfast soon got her going. The meal was a quiet affair compared to the night before. Alice was already out in the stables and everyone else seemed full of sleep like her, and focused on their fried eggs and bacon.

After eating, Beth took herself to the indoor riding school, as Alice had instructed. She saw Paula walking happily across the yard on Sarah's arm and watched their group togetherness in envy.

Alice was already there, with a saddled JR, who was docile, even without her holding him. She was scratching his neck and murmuring something in his ear that Beth couldn't hear. When they noticed Beth, she stopped and said 'hi' and, without preamble, she continued, 'I sense that you are not comfortable around horses, Beth.'

It wasn't a question but she seemed to pause in expectation of an answer. Beth just made a non-committal 'mmm' sound.

'But,' Alice continued, 'I also sense that you are a horse woman.'

Beth was dumbfounded and simply stood in her place about five feet away from them.

'In order to ride a horse, the first thing you need to do is build a rapport. JR senses your unease just as I do: do you see how his relaxed body language changed as you came in?' Beth noticed that Alice was now holding his reins but otherwise saw no difference. 'He has stiffened up', Alice continued, 'and is more anxious.'

Beth felt terrible, she wanted to leave. Was she really making the horse anxious just by standing there?

'It's not your fault, Beth, horses are instinctive, but you can learn to trust each other. JR needs to know that you are relaxed with him and not a threat, this is the reason why he is tense.'

'Right,' Beth managed, doing her breathing.

'Deep breathing is good,' Alice noted. Beth was surprised that she had picked up on it. 'Come closer to JR.'

Beth took a step nearer.

'No, come close, stand in front of his face.'

Beth felt she had no choice.

'JR will never hurt you, he is a gentleman.' She scratched his neck again with real affection. 'Now, hold out you hand like this,' she held out her hand palm down, fingers neutral and slightly bent downwards, 'let him sniff your hand and he will know that you are not going to hurt him either. If you came at him to pat him before you show him you are passive, he may worry and misread you. Horses don't like to have their faces touched too much, try to pat his neck.'

Beth held out her hand and JR nuzzled it.

'Now,' Alice watched approvingly, 'continue your deep breathing through your nose. Let him feel your breaths.'

Beth felt silly but she forced herself not to glance round to check if anyone was looking, then breathed slowly in and out. JR stood calmly and started to breathe with her, his nose almost against hers.

After a moment or two, Alice whispered, 'See, you are communicating!'

Beth could see and she reached out to scratch his neck as he leaned into her. She saw a flash out of the corner of her eye. Alice was holding up her phone and had taken a shot. She showed it to Beth. JR had his nose against her chest and she was holding him and smiling. She looked at Alice in awe.

'See!' Alice clapped her hands. 'It took you less than five minutes for JR to connect with you and see your soul. He sees that you are good, a friend. I'll email that photo to you.'

Beth looked at JR – his big black soulful eyes were looking at her. Alice took a pony nut from her pocket and handed it to Beth, 'Here, give him that.'

Beth remembered to place it in her open palm and hold it out to him and his lips soon gobbled it from her hand.

He sees that I am good, Beth repeated to herself, and Alice seemed to sense these thoughts as she said: 'Horse's brains are not as sophisticated or anywhere near as large as human brains, of course: we have three important areas and horses have two. They can't plan things, make decisions about things, use language and so on the way we do, but they do have memory and they can feel emotion. They are like dogs in that they can know a person quickly. They are often dismissed as acting only on herding instinct but I see that JR knows you are good and next time he sees you, he will recognise you. All you need to do is keep him trusting you.'

She scratched him again and snuggled her face into his mane before saying: 'Okay, I think you're both ready for you to get up in the saddle now and then I'll show you how to sit, how to hold the reins and communicate with him when he can't see you. Lastly, we'll all walk around the ring so that you can get a feel of walking, then it will be break time. Okay?'

'Yes, that's okay,' Beth nodded and smiled again, surprised by how calm she felt at the idea and how she felt she knew that she was going to enjoy it.

Alice gave her JR's reins to hold as she demonstrated how to mount the horse. Beth wasn't sure how much of what Alice had said she actually believed to be true, but she felt safe here.

Chapter 27

When Beth got to the kitchen for tea break, she was the last person to arrive. As soon as she walked in, everyone went quiet, as if they had just been talking about her. Paula was sitting cosied up with the other three and Sarah was pouring tea as usual from a big pot. Joe was leaning on the sink next to Alice, who still had her back to the room.

As Beth sat down, unsure whether to join the huddle at the end, so deciding on the seat at the other end from where she could see everyone, Joe pulled down the window blinds and the room went dim. Alice turned round and held out a cake with two sparklers in the top and everyone else started signing 'Happy Birthday', looking at Beth as they signed. Paula must have taught them all to do it. As they neared the end, they didn't sign 'happy birthday dear Beth' as a closed fist circling the chest to sign sorry but 'happy birthday dear Beth' as a slightly bent index finger making a small slow circle around the temple in the sign for 'thoughtful'.

When they had finished and were waving their hands in the deaf visual way of clapping, Sam spoke and simultaneously signed the words he knew for Paula's benefit. 'Paula changed your name-sign to "thoughtful". She said that when she gave you the name "sorry" it wasn't a real name-sign as she had to think of one quickly before she really knew you. Now she thinks this suits you a lot better.'

> *Yes, yes,* signed Paula, *you always think how you can support deaf people and are a fantastic advocate for us. You never make my decisions for me.*

Beth had mixed feelings. The attention bothered her and how much was Sam behind this name change? She felt pleased and wary in turn.

Before she had time to respond, Alice said: 'I got your date of birth from your application form. Joe and I thought we'd surprise you with a cake.' The two of them were now sitting side by side at the table and Joe had cut the cake into hearty, equal slices. Alice took hold of his hand and grinned at him adoringly then spoke to the group: 'We'll have a little ride in the field before lunch and then untack the horses to rest them up for our afternoon hack down to the lake. Beth and JR got on really well. Look!' She got her phone from her pocket and showed them all the photo. Beth saw a knowing glance pass between Sam and Sarah. What was it now?

When they went out to get their horses, fireman Sam left his wheelchair in the house. It was odd to see him walking on his long, slightly gangly legs. He was drowned in too-loose dark brown jodhpurs and a thick puffy riding jacket. They discovered that Vicky had already re-saddled all five horses as they took them from the stables. Beth greeted JR with a passive hand and a neck scratch as she lead him to the yard. There was a mounting block with a ramp for wheelchair users. Sam and Paula both used the block to get on their horses.

Everyone but Beth was in jodhpurs and was sitting up straight and confident on their horses. Beth felt dowdy in her old corduroy trousers, which were digging into her waist and felt too tight around her crotch. She tried to sit straight like the others.

Izzy had tied her hair back from her face for the first time, and she seemed to relax in her horse's company, knowing, perhaps, that he'd probably not see her mutilated face and would probably not react to it if he did. Beth realised that Izzy's mum wasn't here yet: perhaps she was coming later in the day?

They set off, with Vicky walking by Paula and her small, grey horse. Vicky wasn't leading them but instead walked close as they left the yard and followed a track to the gate that Alice was opening into a field, ready to grab the reins should Paula go off track. At the moment, the lovely little horse was gracefully following the others and taking note of where Vicky was walking.

Beth looked about her and breathed deeply, cold air cleansing her lungs. She closed her eyes and felt the sun on her skin. Even though it had minimal warmth to it, she felt it playing on her face. Sam and Izzy were leading the group and walked their horses side by side, chatting easily together. Beth could hear the odd phrase; they were talking about horses and the horse that Izzy's family had owned when she was growing up.

Without all of her lips, Izzy's speech was slurred and unclear in a similar way to Paula's deaf voice. She couldn't form sounds that involved bringing the lips together: The letters *p* and *b* eluded her, *f* and *v* were almost as indecipherable but, with careful listening, you could understand her. Sam seemed to have no problem. Perhaps earlier he had found a way to bring her out of her shell and had had time to familiarise himself with her voice.

Alice asked them to walk their horses in a circle, leaving space between each horse. She didn't single people out but shouted instructions to everyone: 'shorten your reins now', 'engage the horse's attention', 'keep your heads turned in the direction you're asking the horse to go', 'keep your heels down', 'sit up straight', 'shoulders back'.

They stopped, walked to her, changed direction, walked around the edge of the field and diagonally across it, turning their heads and shoulders in the direction they were going and only pulling gently on the reins.

The time in the field passed quickly and Beth was disappointed when Alice announced that it was lunch time and they headed back to the farm.

Joe gave them all a mug of steaming hot, spicy parsnip soup, served with wholemeal rolls fresh from the oven. Paula sat next to Beth again and asked her how she was enjoying it. Fireman Sam was quiet as he ate, mumbling that he needed to 'refuel'. To Beth's surprise, Izzy sat opposite Paula at their end of the table, asking Paula about signs for various things relating to horses and food. She had already picked up fingerspelling and seemed to really love the signing. She looked a lot more relaxed and happy, keeping her hair tied back to expose her face fully.

Beth felt she should make contact with her, and spoke and signed to ask when her mum was arriving. Izzy's face darkened for a second. 'I can manage without my mum, you know?' she snapped, sounding more like a petulant 14–year–old than a young adult. Beth saw the fighter in her, the girl who wanted to be allowed to grow up again now that everyone was mollycoddling her.

'Yes, sure, it's just that Alice mentioned your mum might come,' Beth said, trying to sound not in the least patronising.

Izzy didn't apologise but, obviously recognising her abruptness, she asked Paula how to sign 'change of plan' and signed that to Beth before she spoke again. 'I rang her and told her not to bother coming.'

Beth sensed that they'd probably had an agreement that Izzy would see how she got on before deciding if her mum should come or not. She kept her mouth shut after that, scared of offending the girl more. She'd been to get her phone from her room before lunch and now got it out from her pocket. Sure enough, her dad had called but left no message. There was also a text message from Rick that read simply *happy birthday*, which she'd acknowledge later in equally benign language. She excused herself, went out to the porch and dialled her dad's number.

'Hello?'

He picked up on the fourth ring.

'Hello, Dad, it's Beth.'

'Oh hello,' he sounded surprised that it was her but Beth didn't allow her hackles to rise instantly. What Rick had said about Vivien liking him enough to have a baby with him had made her think that perhaps she had been hearing inflections that weren't there. Her dad had always hated phones.

Beth waited but he didn't speak further so she asked, 'How's Lucy?'

'Lucy? How did you know her name?'

'You told me, Dad.'

'Ah.' Pause again, 'Lucy is fine, she cries a lot, like you did.' A rare reference to Beth's provenance.

'So…' she added.

'So…' There was more silence for a moment, 'Oh yes, happy birthday.'

'Thanks, Dad,' she sighed, scratching her head, 'well, I have to go.'

'Go where?'

'I have to hang up, I'm on holiday.'

'You are?!' he sounded disbelieving but maybe he just came across wrong on the phone.

'I am, I have to go, Dad, thanks for calling earlier though, I thought you might not.'

'It's your birthday!'

'I know but…' She didn't want to remind him of the *please daddy* comment. 'Just we have already spoken more than usual recently.'

'That is true.'

'I have to go, Dad, sorry, but maybe I could call you again soon to hear how Lucy is?'

'Yes, okay.'

'Okay, Dad, I will.'

She hung up, feeling a sense of jubilation. Perhaps things could improve with her dad? This place was already doing her good.

When Beth got back to the warm kitchen and its smells of home baking and fresh bread, Alice stood up and rattled a spoon in her soup mug:

'The afternoon hack will start at 2pm, it might take between two and three hours. Joe will drive out on the quad bike later and meet us at the lake with flasks of tea and some cookies. When we're riding, I won't say too much, you can just relax and enjoy the views. Remember you can slacken your reins and give your horses their heads to let them stretch their necks a bit. When we get back, Vicky and I will bed down the horses if you are tired, but if you'd like to help us, you're very welcome.

'Wrap up warm, it's getting blustery. Remember that scarves should be tucked inside jackets and everything must be done up so nothing flaps and spooks any of the horses. You'll be riding the same horses you were on this morning. Any questions?'

There were none. They had a bit of time so Beth and Paula went to their room for a lie down before the big ride.

You'll love it, Paula signed, *I can't even see that much of the view but I can tell it's beautiful.* Beth believed her on both counts.

Chapter 28

Sam was worn out but not exhausted in the way he got sometimes. He was making sure that he got plenty of food, knowing that food is fuel to the body. There was certainly no shortage of food here.

The hack out was pretty quiet, each rider lost in their thoughts. He looked around at one point and wondered what each of them was thinking. They all looked free, faces relaxed as they swayed gently in sync with their horse's gait. Beth looked a little self-conscious in her tatty old cords and lumpy raincoat. His horse ended up walking beside JR at one point and he managed a brief conversation with her, not really getting beyond the weather, the cold and the beautiful countryside, but that was a start. She'd barely said two words to him all day otherwise. He seemed to have offended her at some stage.

In an odd way, Sam was pleased at what he felt was her open animosity toward him. He'd found since his illness, especially when he was using the chair, that he was greeted with sympathetic smiles everywhere he went, no matter what he was doing. Whatever he did, he'd get the 'Aww, isn't he cute!' look. He didn't mind the smiles, and felt oddly secure in them now, but his wicked side sometimes wanted to do bad things to see how far he could push people before they lost 'the look'. He felt, sometimes, that people put up with him just because they felt they should humour the crip and not because they really liked him. Beth was different. She seemed to have no such compunctions, disliking him with no regard to his disabilities.

When they got to the lake and dismounted to rest, Joe quadbiked out as promised, with a brown-paper bag full of freshly baked cookies and flasks of tea. Everyone was so much at peace that they just relaxed against a dry-stone wall and looked out at the calming waters.

As they were all totally worn out by the time they got back,

Alice and Vicky were out of luck getting any help to bed down the horses, but Joe's dinner of beef stew and dumplings was devoured in no time. Again, there was little by way of conversation, but Sam did find the energy to suggest meeting for hot drinks and a few hands of cards at eight and everyone was keen. Probably, like him, they wanted to keep the atmosphere of togetherness going a while longer.

Sam knocked on Sarah's door at 7.55pm.

She came at once. 'Okay, let's go!' she said. 'Did you bring the cards?'

'Check, sir,' he saluted and followed her up the corridor.

'Did you get some rest?'

'Check, sir,' he saluted again to her back.

'Good, you're ready to be fleeced then.'

'I'm ready, hope you are.'

Beth and Paula were already in the kitchen; he hadn't expected that. They were signing and he spotted the sign for 'football' amongst the rest. As they sat down, Paula signed to him,

Donna's 'something' won the cup.

He didn't quite get it. He knew that the sign 'spiky-hair' was her girlfriend's name-sign but he didn't understand the sign that brought both hands together to form a circle.

What? He copied the circular hands sign.
R–O–V–E–R–S ladies.

He was flummoxed for a second but then realised that she'd thought he was asking something else.

Erm, I don't understand what that sign means?
T–e–a–m.
Oh right, I understand! Wow, brilliant.

He was a bit too tired to try to communicate in sign and wished Beth would help, but she seemed happy to leave them to it. Izzy hadn't yet arrived and, as he'd been waiting for the chance to ask Paula something else, he tried signing again:

Sign what, s-u-f-f-e-r-i-n-g?

Paula held both hands in front of her, fingers splayed, palms facing her body and she shook her hands up and down, like the sign he'd already learned for pain.

You know you have Usher? he asked her; rhetorically, he thought, but Paula hesitated.
Erm, for some reason she glanced at Beth, *I'm deaf-blind, yes.*
Do you think you suffer from being deaf-blind?

Paula didn't pause at all to give her answer:

No, I don't suffer. Do you suffer from MS?

Sam paused too: he had thought about this a lot. He'd love to say an outright 'no', like Paula, because he didn't like the word and he didn't like the pity it conjured. Sometimes, though, he wondered.
  'Beth?' he asked, 'Would you mind signing this while I talk, I don't know the signs.'
  Beth showed none of the irritation he'd noticed at other times. Instead, she nodded and tapped Paula's arm:

I'll sign for fireman Sam now while he talks.
Okay, Paula consented with a smile.

Sam could smell alcohol on Beth's breath, and her eyes were slightly glassy. He continued:
  'I think,' he proclaimed, in an obviously well thought-out pitch, 'that suffering is quite an individual thing. You can take two people and give them the same challenges or problems; one person might suffer and the other might not.' He stopped to allow Beth to catch up and to see if Paula responded. She didn't but waited for him to

go on. 'Suffering can also depend on the situation. For example, this weekend I am definitely not suffering from my MS. Without MS, I'd probably never've started riding and I almost certainly wouldn't be here to have such a lovely day so it's almost the opposite of suffering, don't you think?'

Paula nodded enthusiastically.

'But sometimes,' he went on, 'when I'm having a very bad day, am alone in my flat and in pain, I think maybe I am suffering. I mean I don't like to be labelled a sufferer. I'd rather be a struggler, if that's a word, or someone who is learning to live with a difficult thing. I hate MS but I don't want to be a victim to it.'

'Does admitting that you're suffering imply that you are a victim?' Sarah chipped in.

'I think that by allowing yourself to suffer something difficult, you're letting yourself be a victim to it, yes.'

He was interested to hear what Paula and Beth had to say.

You think what, Paula? He signed.

I agree, it's how you live with something that defines you as a sufferer or not. I hate the label and the assumption we suffer all the time.

Beth voiced that.

Yes, exactly, Sam signed. Then he spoke, looking at Beth:

'Shit happens to nearly everyone in life, probably everyone full stop, but how it affects you and whether or not you suffer from it can depend a lot on the person. Would you agree?'

Beth gave a slight nod and that was all he needed to plough on with his theories.

'I mean, I'm not criticising anyone who does suffer. I think different personality types deal with things in different ways. Often, though, it's only through great hardship that we can find our strength. Things that look like unassailable setbacks to people not affected by them can become positive challenges to people when they are forced to deal with them.'

Beth signed to Paula, often needing to go back and clarify things or fingerspell a word.

I agree, Paula finally replied.

'What do you think, Beth?'

'I'm signing for Paula, I can't do both things at once,' she said and signed, returning to her curt defensiveness.

It's okay, speak and sign, you can always tell me later, Paula encouraged.

Sure?

Yes.

Beth took a breath. Sam hoped her tongue might be loosened by whatever it was she had been drinking, but all she said was, 'I'm not sure I can comment really, since I don't have a disability.'

'But suffering goes way beyond disability. We all have hardship in life, traumas. What's yours, Beth, you must have one or more?'

Beth didn't answer and looked at her hands on the table. Sam didn't want to press her and instead asked, 'It doesn't matter what it is, but what do you think about feeling suffering from trauma? Do you think it's inevitable or avoidable?'

Beth was breathing in and out of her nose slowly. Sam recognised that calming technique. He smelled stale wine again. 'Are you okay, Beth? No need to answer if you…' He tailed off as he wanted her to answer but felt a cad for having upset her.

'I'm not sure I agree,' she said finally. 'I mean, some people seem to have so many hard things that there is nothing they can do but suffer. It's like pow, pow, pow.' She made a gun with her hand and, Sam noted, pointed it at her own head.

'I didn't mean to sound glib,' he said.

'No, no, I know what you mean, but I just think that sometimes you can't always choose yourself how much a trauma will make you suffer.'

'Go on.'

'Well, how much and if you suffer can be affected by circum-stance, other people, the timing of things, the severity...'

Sam could sense her pain and hoped that he hadn't sounded too pompous and self-righteous. After all, it had taken him years to break out from feeling like a suffering victim to his MS. He wanted to reassure her.

'I don't mean you can choose instantly how something will affect you, it's not that I think you always have a choice, I just mean some people seem to survive better than others when they have an inbuilt survivor spirit.' Beth didn't look at all assuaged so he tried again. 'I know mental strength isn't something you can just decide on and manipulate yourself.'

He looked at Beth. He seemed to be making her inner turmoil worse.

He laughed to lighten the mood. 'Sorry, I'm making a pig's ear of this! I do think everyone's stronger than they think when they have to deal with something, I guess that's what I'm trying to say. Or maybe not?! I've lost the plot now!' He looked to get off the sub-ject and remembered her name-sign. He signed and smiled.

Name you Beth-thoughtful, I understand why now.

Paula clapped, although she can't have got all of what was said-signed.

'You think about things a lot, don't you?' Sam added. He didn't want to patronise her so he smiled in a way he hoped was relaxed. He'd love to carry on this conversation because he loved philosophi-cal arguing. He had been known to say the opposite to what he truly believed just to keep an argument going. He rarely got the chance to talk like this. Danny at the MS centre sometimes humoured him and Frida never shied from an intellectual debate but he didn't get that much chance to really talk with either of them. However, he couldn't see how to press on with this one without making Beth clam up even more.

Luckily, just then Izzy walked in, wearing her pyjamas and dress-ing gown and carrying a pack of Uno cards. He was saved from try-ing to think what to say next.

'Sorry I'm not dressed, guys, it will be an early night for me,' Izzy announced.

'For all of us, I should think,' said Sam, noting how very relaxed she had become in such a short time.

Sarah got up and reboiled the kettle, taking orders for hot drinks. Alice and Joe were in their own little private apartment tonight, leaving the guests to themselves.

Izzy asked if everyone knew Uno and it turned out that they'd all played at one time or another. They started simple, adding more and more rules as they went along, some of them ridiculous. The game suited everyone as it was clear and easy. Paula taught them all to sign the colours: blue, red, green and yellow. At first, Izzy won too easily, she was obviously experienced, but as time went on, it got closer, tighter, faster. They all laughed together when someone ended up picking up about twenty cards.

Sam watched everyone focusing, laughing, cheeks glowing, and the kitchen windows begin to steam up. This is what he knew would happen if only he could get everyone to sit down to a game. Playing cards was always the answer and he vowed to himself to buy his own set of Uno cards when he got home.

When Izzy and Paula went to bed and Sarah popped to the loo, he and Beth were left alone in the kitchen. Feeling that the barriers that had prevented them talking were finally starting to come down, he stole the moment to ask gently what she had been drinking.

'I had a bottle of wine in my room.'

She looked embarrassed but not offended that he'd asked, no doubt mellowed by wine and the camaraderie of the evening. There were patterns from his own experiences that he could see: bringing wine but keeping it hidden, not sharing it, drinking it surreptitiously. It brought things to his mind that he didn't particularly want to remember but felt he wanted to share with her. He also felt that it might allow her to open up more, knowing he had been through something similar. It was a bit of a gamble, bringing it up without much preamble, but they didn't have much time before Sarah would be back.

'After I was diagnosed with MS, I soon lost my job and as good as lost my partner and son. I got thrown into a terrible depression and felt the world was closing in on me.' Beth nodded and he knew she really understood. 'I used to shut myself away, eating terrible food, drinking too much and generally hiding in my cave of grief. It was a feeling that no one could possibly understand what I was going through.'

Beth looked about to speak, eyes fixed on his, when Sarah came back too soon and started clearing up the mugs, unknowingly breaking the atmosphere he felt building between them. He had a swell of tenderness for her that surprised him, a flicker of kinship.

When they all got up to go to bed, he felt disappointed, craving more time with her and wondering if they would get another chance to be alone together.

Chapter 29

Sunday morning was wet so they rode indoors before settling down to Joe's huge Sunday roast, their finale lunch, where there was much laughter and relaxed chatter before packing up.

As they stood in the car park watching Joe put their cases in the boot, Beth thought how different things were from when they had arrived on Friday to be greeted by the disappearing back of a man in a wheelchair and the smiling 'hello' of a fresh-faced, grinning woman. She remembered finding an excuse to loiter so that she could avoid talking to them in reception. She remembered being greeted by a tall, broad-shouldered man with a pony-tail. She picked out that moment as the one when she had started, little by very little, to relax.

She had only started to see last night, over cards and group laughter, how relaxed and open Sam seemed to be. She felt a little ashamed of her immediate suspicions of him. Watching him find ways to draw Izzy out and to communicate with Paula, she'd felt a sense of something close to pride. She also saw that he was doing the same with her: quietly and patiently learning what was inside her. The conversation he had started at the end of the evening proved it to her. She so wished it could have developed.

Now that she had his phone number and email address stored firmly in her own handset, she was sure that they had only just brushed the surface of the talking they had to do together. It was funny, some people – most people – she was suspicious of for a long time, but with the group here, influenced by Alice and Joe's relaxed welcome, she'd begun to gel and bond. Izzy was like a different person after such a short time and Beth hoped that she could get back to riding and being around horses more often, and that she'd also find the right people to spend time with.

She was very sad to be going home and didn't want to think about the week ahead, closing it off for a while longer and feeling eternally grateful to Paula for bringing her here and to Donna for not being able to come.

As they drove away, Beth felt a sudden wave of loneliness and was hit by the depressing thought of returning to her silent, empty house. That morning, on a whim, she'd given the last bottles of wine to Alice and Joe as a thank-you gift. She determined not to buy more.

The journey home went very well. It being Sunday afternoon, the roads were quiet even when they hit more urban areas and they drove without stopping. As she pulled up at Paula's, the front door opened, and Donna stood in the threshold waving as Barney dashed around her legs and raced over to the car. Donna came out and flung her arms around Paula as if she hadn't seen her in years. They kissed then, mouths locked together passionately. Beth looked down for Barney but he was jumping up Paula's legs.

It was such a sight of unrestrained love that Beth didn't know what to do. Her stomach seemed to twist up with an emotion she couldn't identify: not really embarrassment, not jealousy, but something else. Yearning, maybe.

> *Thank you, Paula-strong-willed, I had a lovely weekend*, she signed when they eventually pulled apart.
> *Me too, I knew you'd like it there. Thank you for your support, Beth-thoughtful.*

As Beth climbed back in the car, she had tears in her eyes and exhaustion washed over her. She started the car and headed home, with nothing to look forward to but an empty sofa. As she pulled into her road, she saw a car parked outside her house. She knew that car, it was Rick's. As she approached, he got out and leaned against the car, waiting for her to park.

'What is it?' She glanced at her house but saw no damage.

'Can you help me, Beth?'

'What?' She was standing in front of him now; his face looked ashen and his shoulders sagged uncharacteristically.

'Can I stay here? It's Claire, she kicked me out. She convinced herself I was having a fling with you.'

'With me?! Oh God!' Beth put her hands over her eyes as it occurred to her to say, 'But then surely here is the worst place you could be?'

'Might as well prove her right,' he muttered.

Beth didn't know quite what he meant by that, she was so tired.

'Rick, let's go inside, you can stay tonight and we'll talk about it tomorrow.'

'Thanks, Beth, I knew I could count on you.'

Beth bit her lip, not wanting to start a discussion out here in the street.

'Come on, we need a cup of tea.'

'Or this?' Rick said, pulling a bottle of Jack Daniels from his coat. Beth looked at it longingly. There was a difference between not drinking when there was no drink at hand and not drinking when someone wanted to share a bottle with you. She felt her resolve melting away and turned to the house before they could say any more.

While she opened the door, Rick went over to his car and pulled out a bag from the boot. Beth let him in and then went back to her own car to get her things and lock it up safely. She came back to find Rick already in the kitchen, opening the bottle and pouring two generous glasses, his bag abandoned in the hall. Beth mumbled something and took her bag upstairs, throwing it on to the bed and walking to the bathroom. She sat on the loo with her head in her hands feeling that the fates were set against any hope of ever pulling things together.

Chapter 30

When Sam and Sarah set off, they didn't talk much for a long while because Sam fell asleep. After a stop at a gas station for petrol and take-away coffees, Sarah said:

'Oh, I've forgotten to tell you, I rang that man I mentioned about being your PA and he's really keen.'

'Fantastic!'

'Incredible luck, first guy I thought of. His name is Jack, he was a carer for his mum but, I might have said before, she sadly died last year.'

'That takes the shine off it.'

'Yes, but he's very interested and a really nice bloke. I'll give you his number. Anyway, now you're awake, what did you think of the weekend?'

'Loved it. We've been lucky with groupings in the past but, this time, I know I'll stay in touch with everyone.'

'Even me?'

'Even you.' But it was Beth he was thinking about as his eyes started to close again.

When they got to his flat, Sam threw himself on the sofa while Sarah busied herself getting his stuff from the car and opening a few windows to air the place.

'I'll just pop over the road to get milk and make you a cup of tea before I go,' she shouted from the hall.

'You're a star.'

He got his phone out, seeing that he'd missed a call from Ollie while he'd been asleep. The voicemail message said: 'Hi, Dad, have you had a good weekend? I went to Chester Zoo with Mum and Enrico. He bought me a cool monkey bag. Talk soon.'

He felt such a stab at the thought of the three of them out together playing happy families that his eyes started watering. He couldn't bring himself to ring Ollie straight back and hear all about his great day out, not in the exhausted state he was in. What sort of dad did that make him?

Sarah bought him a cup of sugary tea and sat next to him, noticing the tears.

'Are you okay? What's happened?'

'Oh, it's nothing. Ollie had a great day out with Kim and Enrico.' He said 'Enrico' in a false and exaggerated Italian accent.

'That's bound to hurt.'

'Just got to me.' He shook his head. 'Good news Ols had a nice day, I guess. I'm feeling so tired, I'd cry at anything. I'll be okay, you get off, I bet you're dying to see your amour.'

'I am! Are you sure you're okay? I bought some eggs and bread, too, but do you need me to get more food for tomorrow?'

'No, Mother, my freezer is full and you are not on my books any more.'

'Pfft, as long as you're sure you're okay.'

'I'm sure, I just need a rest. I was like this last time, flopping as soon as I got home.' He knew he'd be in for at least a few days recovering.

'Well, it was a wonderful weekend, thank you so much.' She hugged him warmly. 'I'll ring you later to see how you're doing and we'll go for coffee soon.'

As soon as she left, he lay down on the sofa, feet hanging over the arm, breathing as calmly as he could and shutting his eyes. It *had* been a wonderful weekend and getting frustrated and upset now wouldn't help anyone.

Chapter 31

When Beth finally went downstairs, having sat on the loo as long as she could, then pulling clothes to wash from her case, Rick was on the sofa with a half-empty bottle next to him and both the glasses were full. He must have been on his second or third by now and sat slumped in the cushions.

'I'm going to get a cup of tea,' Beth shouted from the door, 'want one?'

'No thanks, this'll do.' And he picked up his glass. 'Come and have a drink with me, Beth.'

She didn't want to start drinking, she'd been breathing and putting herself and Paula in the warm, happy kitchen with Izzy-long hair, Sarah-laugh and fireman Sam. She was going to stay there as long as she could.

'I'll just get one,' she said, deliberately taking the words 'a drink' in the literal sense.

As soon as she sat on the sofa, Rick started talking, 'I don't know why she got the idea. I've been a good husband.'

Beth bit her lip and sipped her tea.

Rick sighed. 'It was the text.'

'What text?'

'The birthday one.'

'What, when you texted me on Saturday? All you said was *happy birthday*, it was hardly X-rated.'

'I know, but I forgot her birthday last month. She was furious that we've been married so long and I still forgot her birthday but I remembered yours. I've never seen her so mad.'

'Why did she see the text?'

'She said she looked; she needed "confirmation of what she suspected". She packed my bag for me while I was pleading with her that she'd got it all wrong.'

'Had she?' Beth couldn't resist saying. There was no flirtation in

151

her voice: any wanting she'd felt toward Rick was dead; it had been the drink on both sides, she knew.

'Well, I know you and me did it but we're not all dewy-eyed and amorous, are we?'

'No.' Beth said flatly. 'So tonight you can stay in my house but it'll have to be the sofa again. This can't be too long-term, Rick, but I feel you'll work it out with Claire.'

'You didn't see her.'

'Well, she'll calm down and you can talk to her... calmly.'

'If you say so, you're a woman so I guess you know more about women than I do.' He paused and sighed and put his drink down, then suddenly flung himself at her, butting her nose with his head as he launched to kiss her.

'Stop it, Rick, STOP!' She pushed him away and, to his credit, he pulled back and slumped again, head in hands.

'Oh God, oh God, I'm sorry, Beth, I'm sorry.' His voice was breaking up but she felt emotionally numb.

She stood up. 'I'll make you a coffee,' she said and left the room, picking up the bottle of JD on her way and pouring what was left down the sink.

When she got back, Rick was sitting up. 'God, I'm sorry, Beth.'

She handed him the coffee and sat beside him, taking his hand without speaking. Rick slurped his coffee beside her. She'd made it very strong and black with three sugars in it. 'God, Beth! What is that?'

'Sobering–up medicine.'

'I don't know that I want to sober up.'

'I want you to sober up.'

Rick sighed again. 'God, I'm sorry.'

'Stop saying that, Rick, I get it. That was my trick anyway, we must stop throwing ourselves at each other. You'll sort it out with Claire.'

'Right,' he said, still not sounding convinced. 'God, sorry...'

'Rick!'

'No, I mean, God, sorry, I haven't asked about your weekend. You must be knackered. How was it? Are you Lester Piggott yet?'

'It was good, thanks.' She somehow felt reticent about it now, as if the situation here might give it a negative edge. She wanted to maintain the glow she'd felt at Becher's farm.

'That's good,' Rick mumbled, obviously hardly noticing or caring. 'I'll buy us a Chinese for tea,' he said randomly changing the subject, 'least I can do.'

'Okay,' she breathed and shut her eyes.

Rick got up then. 'I need a piss,' he informed her, swaying out of the room and leaving Beth to fall back into the sofa. She heard him scrabbling through his bag in the hall. Was he searching for loo roll? Who knew.

Her phone rang: it was Sam. Beth felt herself blushing as she answered. 'Hi, Beth here.'

'Hi, Beth, it's Sam, erm, just ringing to check you got home okay?'

'I did. You?'

'Yes, I slept practically the whole way home and have just had another good hour. I'm friends with Paula and Izzy on Facebook now, they're fine, erm…' He sounded awkward.

'That's good, I don't use Facebook.' Beth wanted to break through the ice that seemed to be back between them. She wanted to talk properly but somehow it felt incongruous, misplaced. Sam was from somewhere else, not reality. All this Rick stuff had thrown her back into her other world. Right on cue, Rick shouted down the stairs, 'Have you got a spare toothbrush, Beth? Mine's not in my bag.' She didn't know what to say.

'Sorry,' she mumbled to Sam, 'hang on.' 'I'm on the phone!' she called up to Rick, putting her hand over the mouthpiece.

'Oh right, sorry.' He shut up.

'Sorry, Sam.' She wanted to explain, to tell Sam it was only Rick, but where could she start? *It's just Rick, my ex workmate. We had drunken sex that I can't even remember and now his wife has kicked him out.* Is that what she should say?

'Sounds like you have company, I didn't realise, sorry,' Sam blustered.

'No, no it's fine, I…' She paused, words stuck in her throat.

'I'll go, Beth, maybe talk to you another time. Glad you got back okay anyway.' Sam sounded flat, at a loss about what to say.

'Okay, thank you, another time would be good.' She felt inhibited.

'Goodnight then.'

'Night.'

He hung up, Beth felt like crying. At that moment, she resented Rick so much that she wanted to go upstairs and beat his brains out. She fell back on the sofa and reached for her untouched glass of Jack Daniels, taking several gulps without tasting it.

'Who was it?' asked Rick, coming back in the room.

'Just someone from the weekend checking I'd got home okay.'

'Oh right, that's nice.' He flopped down next to her.

'Changed your mind then?' he said, pointing to her glass. 'I think I'll have another.' Beth said nothing and waited for the inevitable.

'Where's the bottle?'

'I took it away, you'd had enough.'

'Where is it?'

She hesitated a second, 'In the kitchen.'

'Oh right,' and he got up, 'I'll get it.'

'I tipped it down the sink,' she mumbled.

'You did what?!'

'You'd had enough.'

'Jesus, Beth, aren't I allowed to get plastered on the night my wife kicks me out?'

'Here, look, finish this,' and she handed him her half-drunk glass.

'Have you got anything else?'

'No, Rick, I've been away.' Why did she feel she was the one in the wrong?

'I'll go to the shop.'

'Don't, Rick.' But he was up again, pulling on his coat. 'Can you ring the Chinese while I'm out? I'm starving. I'll have sweet and sour pork with fried rice and get some prawn crackers.' With that, he was gone and she had half a mind to lock him out. She had a headache and went to get some pills, downing two glasses of water. She didn't want takeaway, all she wanted was bed.

Nevertheless, she found the number for the nearest Chinese and rang in Rick's order, then she went to get some bedding and a towel for him and found a toothbrush still in its packet. What was she doing running around like a servant in her own house?

She heard Rick come back and went downstairs to give him the stuff and tell him that she had ordered his food and was off to bed. He was pouring himself a massive glass of red wine, said 'okay', not even *thanks,* and went back to sit down. As she went upstairs, she heard the television switching on and tears started to sting her already tired and sore eyes.

Chapter 32

When Beth woke and went downstairs dressed in comfy black clothes for work, Rick was still snoring on the sofa, two empty wine bottles at his feet. She went into the room and switched off the television that he'd left running, leaving the curtains drawn. Unable to face talking to him this early, she was hopeful he'd carry on sleeping.

She had decided to go into college and rang the office to say she'd be in. Lee put on his sympathetic voice and said that was great as long as she felt okay. She wasn't really sure that she did but even college was better than staying at home with Rick here.

She got out her fluoxetine pills. *Today's the day* she heard her mum saying, *no time like the present.* The pills she had were little capsules, half blue and half white. They looked easy to swallow and she downed one with water from the tap, stupidly surprised when she felt nothing, as if she'd been expecting some kind of instant head rush.

She wrote a note for Rick, saying, *left you sleeping, gone to work. You will need to buy some food. Talk to Claire?* and left it on the kitchen table under the jar of coffee and an empty mug. She was serving him again.

At the college, Diane greeted Beth with a nod and then rushed away again, shouting, 'Back in a minute!' over her shoulder. Lee was at his desk taking a phone call. He also nodded to her and held up a finger to say 'one minute', so she stood awkwardly, not knowing what to do as she waited. She got her phone from her bag but there were no texts or messages. She stood idly until Lee put the phone down and stood up.

'Hi, Beth,' he said in a too-jolly voice, giving her a quick hug and then standing back to look at her. 'How *are* you?' he asked.

Beth took a step back too, suddenly feeling hot and suffocated. 'Fine, thanks,' she managed, trying to smile, 'how are *you*?'

Paula had taught her that trick. If anyone asked you a question that made you uncomfortable, the best thing to do was answer as if it was nothing and then ask the same question back to see how they liked it.

'Oh fine, had a good weekend playing golf with my brothers. What did you do?' he added as an afterthought, in a tone that gave away his lack of interest. No doubt he was expecting Beth's normal answer of 'not much really'.

'Oh', said Beth lightly, 'I was on a horse–riding weekend support-ing a deaf–blind friend of mine.'

Lee looked temporarily thrown and tossed his head back in disbe-lief but when he got control of himself said, 'Really? Wow. I didn't know you rode.'

'I don't.'

Beth was quite enjoying this now, watching his face swinging between perplexity and feigned nonchalance.

She wanted to tell him more but Diane came back then and Lee soon disappeared in a fluster.

'I'll put you in with Becky again today. I just saw Gail heading down to the room so you can get a lesson plan before you start. Okay?' Diane was as brisk as ever, not even asking how Beth was.

'Yes, okay.' *Here we go*, Beth thought to herself and headed out of the office.

It might have been Beth's imagination, as she'd only taken one pill, but she felt her heart fluttering, a kind of nervousness she felt could be a precursor to anxiety of a worse kind. When she'd had pills previously, she remembered having weeks of out–of–control wor-rying. Everything had panicked her: she fretted if someone was two minutes late, if she didn't know exactly what she'd be doing and when. Any kind of uncertainty or change from 'normal' had freaked her out. She hoped that these new pills would be a bit different, help her to feel more calm from the outset. These flutters of nervousness didn't bode too well.

She followed Gail to the classroom.

'Morning, Gail, I'm signing for Becky today. What's the plan?' Beth used her usual phrase to sound casual and light-hearted and Gail seemed to buy it.

'Hi, Beth, Becky's group is in here first today and the treatment room in the afternoon. We're going through these from last week,' she indicated a pile of what looked like question papers, 'and then, depending on time, two or three students are giving an oral presentation on an alternative therapy of their choice.'

Beth closed her eyes and breathed, thinking of the warm kitchen, panic rising in her that she might not handle this.

'Okay,' she said in a too-bright voice, not even bothering to ask if the students had been told to bring copies of their notes for the person signing. She already knew the answer would be negative.

As expected, there were no notes to look through and no time even to ask the students the topic of their presentations. Beth listened to Jackie talking about colour therapy and how 'amazing' it was. There was quite a lot to sign and even more for Zoe's session on acupuncture. Both presentations were followed by question and answer, which was always difficult for Becky. Beth's signing inevitably had a time lag, as she listened and then turned the speech into BSL, so Becky missed the normal pauses between questions. By the time they had caught up and Becky was ready to ask something, another student had already got in with a new question.

As Beth was packing up, Gail came over and said how beautiful and clear her signing was. Beth always considered this reaction from a non-signing person ridiculous. She could have been ignoring the presentations and signing Humpty Dumpty for all Gail knew. She tried to smile and muttered thanks as she got out of the classroom as quickly as she could.

She couldn't face talking to anyone in the canteen and so decided to go and get some air. What she wanted most was a glass of wine. As she was going down the corridor, Gemma stepped out of a classroom into her path.

'Oh *hi*, Beth,' she grinned, 'How are *you*?'

This was clearly going to be a theme but Beth had no fight in her. 'Oh you know, tired,' she replied. And with that she moved to step by, but instead felt a hand on her arm.

'Lee says you have been on a riding weekend? I love horses!'

God, it hadn't taken him long. Beth wondered what else they'd said. *I thought she was too ill to work. She doesn't look like the horse-rid-ing type. Who's her 'friend'?*

'I was supporting a deaf-blind friend.'

'Really?' Gemma looked impressed, 'I worked with a deaf-blind lady recently, talk about hard work!'

'Oh, I enjoyed it.' Beth badly wanted to go outside but Gemma kept on talking in her pally, sing-song way.

'When I was working with Paula, she had a real chip on her shoulder and couldn't accept help at all.'

Beth's stomach flipped.

'Paula?'

'Yes, her name was Paula. Oh God! You might know her, she teaches BSL. Did she teach you? God knows how she manages *that*.' Gemma finally tailed off, seeming at last to pick up on Beth's silence.

'I was away with Paula this weekend,' Beth said curtly.

'Paula Collins?'

'Yes.'

'You're friends with *her*?' It was Gemma's turn to look flustered, 'Wow, you must have a thick skin!'

'When did you work with Paula?'

'Oh, not long ago. I worked for her trial period and then she told me that she didn't think it was the right job for me. Can you believe that?!'

Beth really could.

'I mean, I only applied because she needed help.'

Already a sense of triumph was rising in Beth. It was so good to know that Paula preferred her way of supporting when the college seemed to think that the sun shined out of Gemma's arse.

'I had a lovely weekend,' she repeated. 'Excuse me, I need to go to my car,' and with that she pushed past a stunned Gemma who, no doubt, would hurry away to find Lee.

Sitting behind the wheel of her car, Beth let out a sigh and put her head back against her slightly too low headrest. College was hard as usual but Gemma's revelation made her glow.

It was hard to believe that it was less than twenty-four hours since she'd pulled out of the yard at Becher's farm. She tried to think about

Alice and Joe and how today they were having a day off before wel-
coming another group of disabled riders tomorrow. The thought
of Izzy, of Sam with his ready smile and Sarah with hers, all sitting
round the table laughing and relaxed, made her glow even more.

Beth felt suddenly fired-up: she would get through today and then
she'd get through tomorrow and the next day.

Feeling buoyed up, she quickly texted Sam: she wanted to explain.
*Sorry I couldn't talk last night, my friend's wife threw him out so he came
to sleep on my sofa. Hope you're rested?*

That would definitely clear things up. She hastily pressed SEND
and headed back to the classroom.

Chapter 33

Sam, Monday

Sam spent the morning drifting between bedroom, kitchen and bathroom. He was aching all over and was now doing some light yoga to stretch out his muscles before lunch. He was also trying to clear his mind but it kept drifting to last night's awkward call to Beth and how wrong he was in assuming that she was single. Of course she had a partner and of course her partner would be there to see her when she got back from a weekend away.

He gently manoeuvred himself from pigeon pose to staff pose, focusing on expanding his chest and lengthening his spine as he breathed smoothly.

His phone beeped: it was a text from Beth. Paula had mentioned that she worked at the college so he guessed it was her lunch break. He read:

Sorry I couldn't talk last night, my friend's wife threw him out so he came to sleep on my sofa. Hope you're rested?

It made him so happy to read that. Her friend's *wife*; slept on her *sofa*. He'd got himself wound up like a schoolboy. What was this fixation he had with Beth? He was about to ring her there and then but caught himself. It was probably better to ring later when college would be over for the day. She might be busy preparing for the afternoon and he didn't want the conversation to be rushed.

Instead, he rounded off his disrupted yoga session with a five-minute corpse pose and then rang his son.

'Dad!'

Oh, it was good to hear Ollie's happy voice.

'Hello, soldier, got time to talk before lunch is over?'

'Yeah, five minutes yet.'

'Sorry I didn't get back to you yesterday, I fell asleep.'

'Thought you might, it's okay.'

'You know me well.' Sam gulped down his pang, knowing that

163

Ollie didn't know him nearly as well as many kids knew their dads. He was certainly perceptive, though.

'Clocked you,' Ollie laughed.

'I missed you over the weekend,' Sam said, bracing himself to add, 'but your trip to the zoo sounded good.'

'It was awesome, the monkeys were hilarious.'

Awesome?

'Cool. I can't wait to hear about it all on Saturday. Hope you got some good photos?' He hoped not too many of them had Enrico in them.

'Yeah, loads on my phone but I haven't uploaded them yet.'

'No worries, show me on Saturday.'

'I will.'

There was nothing Sam wanted more than to say he'd take Ollie to the zoo again. Perhaps he could get his PA to take them both but he'd have to sort out a new PA first. An involuntary sigh escaped him.

'Are you still tired, Dad?'

There was real concern in Ollie's voice.

'Yes, I am, but nothing would stop me ringing my favourite son in his lunch break.'

'Who's your second favourite son?'

'That would be you. You are my least favourite too,' he added, so as not to get mushy and embarrass Ollie.

'You're my favourite and least favourite dad too.' In his tired, worn-out state, Sam nearly choked with emotion. At least Enrico didn't feature on the list.

'I better go, Dad, the bell rang.'

'See you on Saturday.'

They rang off and he rubbed his eyes, feeling washed out.

After a simple lunch of beans on toast, he went to bed again for a couple of hours and fell properly asleep. It was the thought of ringing Beth that got him up. He usually felt groggy after daytime sleeping but today he felt refreshed as he cleaned his teeth and had a shave.

At four, he called her.

'Thanks for your text, Beth, it was good of you to help him out,' he said after the hellos were finished.

'I didn't have much choice, he was camping on my doorstep when I got home!'

'Yeah but still, you must have been knackered.'

'Yes I was, last thing I wanted to come home to.'

'Do you think they'll sort it out?'

'Yeah, I think they will eventually. He's not staying for that long though! I told him he can't.'

'Good for you, sure you need some time to yourself.'

It was good to hear her voice. Yesterday's call had been so awkward.

'Exactly so.'

'Clocked you,' he wanted to say in Ollie-speak but he bit it back.

'How was work?' he said instead.

'Oh, pretty crap. How was your day?'

'Pretty crap.' He felt as if the wall between them had dissolved at last. 'I've been in bed most of the day.'

'Hope that has helped?'

'Yeah, feeling more on top of things already, might even manage a microwave curry.'

'Wow, that good, huh?'

They both chuckled.

'Sorry, but I'd better go and sort out Rick, that's the bloke who has invaded my house.'

'Okay, sure,' he didn't know what to say next, 'speak soon.'

'Yes, speak soon, bye now.'

'See you.'

He knew he would.

Chapter 34

By the time she got home, Beth had almost forgotten about Rick and was only reminded when she saw his car parked on the roadside in front of her house. She half-expected him to still be slumped on the sofa, watching something mind-numbing on TV, wine bottles collecting round his feet. In fact, he was in the kitchen, neatly shaved and smelling of her exotic fruit shampoo.

On her way down the corridor, she had glanced into the living room and seen that all traces of wine bottles were gone, the curtains were open and his bedding was neatly folded on the arm of the sofa.

'Hi, Beth love,' he greeted her, 'how was your day?'

'Exhausting,' she said, throwing herself down in the chair opposite his and noting the sparkling sink and empty draining rack. The fruit bowl on the table had some tasty-looking, firm, yellow bananas in it and a bag of Granny Smiths. He saw her looking.

'I've cleaned up and got you some food in. I feel a right pillock for how I behaved last night.' She hadn't been sure how much of it he would remember.

'Don't worry about it, Rick, I'm surprised you're not still holed up on the sofa. You'd been kicked out of your house!'

'Yeah, I rang Claire, like you said. She's agreed to meet me tomorrow and I'm not going to fight her, whatever she calls me. It's not her fault any of this, is it?'

Beth shook her head.

'I do love her really, you know?'

'I know.'

'I think we'll sort it out and I'll stop being a twat. If she won't take me back tomorrow, I'll go to a hotel or to my mum's.'

Beth was relieved that he'd pulled himself together so well: that was always Rick's way. In his world, he'd roll with the punches and then find a way to mend the bruises.

'That's good, thanks. If Claire knows you're here...'

Rick mimed slicing his neck with his hand and laughed. 'But thanks, mate, I really do owe you.'

Whatever they'd done was over. Beth still couldn't remember that night. As if reading her mind, Rick mused, 'I think I'll tell her everything.'

'Everything as in?'

'We got very pissed and woke up in the same bed but probably nothing happened.'

'Is that the truth?'

'I dunno,' he shrugged. 'To be honest I was lying before, I can't remember jack shit.'

'Nor me.'

'So we might very well have passed out in bed without any shenanigans.'

'We might have.'

Beth was comforted, perhaps that IS what happened. She panicked at the thought of her friend Claire knowing it, knowing how much she drank and that she slept with people's husbands, whether literally or not. 'What's Claire going to say?'

'Don't worry, Claire's been round the block, she'll take it on the chin eventually. She knows people mess up.'

Rick got up and made tea, and Beth was glad that the subject seemed closed, for now.

'You haven't told me much about your trip,' said Rick, taking a swig. 'To be honest, you seem different. Lighter.'

'Lighter?' she pinched the flesh round her middle.

'Lighter in mood, summat's lifted off you.' He paused. 'Reckon it must be love.'

'What must be?'

'Your mood, it's always a bloke, innit? I take it it's not me, so who've you met?'

'Don't be stupid, Rick, I'm not a teenager.'

'You're blushing.'

As soon as he said that, she felt her face getting hot. 'I am now but only because you said I was.'

'If you say so.' There was a pause, 'So what's his name?'

'I met a group of people and enjoyed the horse riding. It was a lovely place.'

'O-kay,' Rick didn't look convinced but seemed about to let her off, before adding, 'I always wanted to be a bridesmaid.'

'Dickhead.' She threw a teaspoon at him.

'Ow, woman, the sooner I get out of this house the better!' He held up his hands in exaggerated defence.

Beth paused. She didn't want to tell him that the reason for her 'lightness of mood' was, more likely, the discovery that Gemma had worked with Paula and not got on with her at all, whereas Paula frequently told Beth how good a PA she was. Beth knew that it would sound completely trivial to anyone else. Let's face it, she thought, it is completely trivial. She noted, too, how much her mood seemed to blow about, based on small events or comments that other people would probably barely take any notice of. She wondered about the pills: did she want to be emotionally zombified? She reckoned that she would try them for a month and see how it went.

Tea finished, Beth went upstairs to shower and change. Wrapping her lavender-scented dressing gown round herself, she immediately felt better. She popped back downstairs to get her mobile from her bag in the hall. There was a message from Sam.

She felt excitement in her stomach but tried to temper it, telling herself not to let her imagination run away with her. She was a grown-up texting a friend but that's not how she felt. *Good to speak just now. Hope things are going okay with Rick. Was thinking, we live close, do you want to call round sometime for a cup of tea and a chat? x*

She stared at the phone, her stomach churning even more. Was he really inviting her to his house? It was unexpected but also felt somehow inevitable that they should meet again. *That would be nice, I could come after work one day? x*

She stayed sitting on her bed waiting for his reply, which came in moments, and they swapped several more texts to sort something out. It turned out that he lived not far from the college and in the end, they agreed that she'd call in on her way home tomorrow after Sam had interviewed a possible new PA.

She was a bit stunned by the rapidity and ease of it and was just beginning to worry about all the things that could go wrong when Rick called up the stairs that tea was ready. She hadn't had her shower but she was feeling just as invigorated.

Chapter 35

Beth, Tuesday

She didn't know what kind of house she'd been expecting Sam to live in but it wasn't this. It was a large detached modern place with at least four bedrooms, surrounded by long, well-tended flower beds and vast, neatly mown lawns. She got out the piece of paper from her pocket and checked the address: this was the right place. Sam said to go round the side and knock on the white door and she followed his instructions.

When she knocked, Sam opened the door quite quickly, with a smile, standing back to let her enter, guiding her with a hand on her back. She felt a small tingle.

'Welcome to fat Sam's grand slam,' he said, laughing, as he mimed jiggling a beer belly.

'Quite a place you have here,' Beth stuttered, but then her eyes adjusted to the dimness after the bright sun outside and she saw that she was in a flat.

'You think?' he said, sweeping his arm around the narrow hall.

'Oh, I see, this is…' Beth felt slightly silly.

'… a granny flat,' he laughed again. 'Quite ironic, really, as the house owners are in their seventies and after the wife's ninety-something mother died, they rented this place out to a bloke almost half their age.'

Beth laughed now. She remembered how relaxed she felt in Sam's company. 'That makes sense, I was imagining you mowing the lawns every morning at five.'

'Not quite,' he said still grinning. 'I do have a little bit of private garden out the back that they fenced off for me. Let's not stand here all day, come through to the lounge. Would you like some coffee? I have a machine for decent stuff.'

'Great, thanks.'

As he went to the kitchen, she looked around the room. On the wall was a framed, A4-sized photo of Sam walking along a beach

171

with a gorgeous little boy sitting on his shoulders, pulling out Sam's ears. A son? A nephew? She couldn't remember if he'd mentioned being a father at the weekend.

She looked for more clues. There was a pair of child-sized shoes half-pushed under the bookshelves opposite her, a shelf dedicated to children's and young adult's books. He must have a boy staying here sometimes but the flat didn't have the air of somewhere a kid lived permanently.

She heard the coffee machine gurgling and Sam poked his head round the door. 'I made macchiato, do you want sugar?'

Beth wasn't exactly sure what a macchiato coffee looked like so she said, 'Yes please, just the one,' in case it was very strong.

There was a book out on the little table by the sofa and she picked it up. It was a book of love poems. She opened it to a book-marked page and read the poem there:

> Sleeping with Angels
> (anonymous)
> In night's deepest stillness, I lie awake and watch you sleeping.
> Your face, lighted by the glow of the streetlamp outside,
> Is facing toward me, beautiful in peaceful repose.
> The corners of your mouth are turned up in a gentle half-smile.
> Beneath my palm, resting on your heart, I feel the rise and fall
> of your slow, even breaths
> And I remember the hours before sleep when our bodies merged,
> Moulding as one and glorying each other.
> In my mind's-eye, I see feathered angel-wings at your back.
> Folded in rest but ready to encircle me again.
> As I watch you lying there, I know what Love looks like.

She read it again and found she had a tear in her eye because that was what she'd missed for so long.

'I like that one,' came Sam's voice as he entered the room in his wheelchair, which he hadn't been using before. Beth looked up.

'Are you okay? Has something happened?'

'Oh this!' he said, bashing his wheel tyres, 'No, it's fine, I brought the chair so I could carry all this in one trip.'

On his knee was a non-slip tray bearing a bowl of nuts, some bananas, and two bottles of water as well as the coffees. Sam put them down on the low table.

'Energy food,' he said with a smile.

'Good plan, you have it all worked out.'

'I try,' he said, looking up. 'I read those poems at night sometimes before sleep. Kind of calming.'

'I wouldn't have had you down as a poetry reader.'

'No? What would you have had me down as?'

'Oh, I don't know, a thriller man?'

'Oh, I read plenty of those too. My mainstay. You should see my Kindle. Do you read?'

'Not that much, I'm usually so tired in the evening, it seems easier just to watch some mindless telly.' She sipped her coffee, it was good.

'I know what you mean, I'm reading a lot more now I have more time at home.'

'I thought the love poems might just be a trick you use for wooing women.'

'Wooing women?!' he laughed and shook his head. 'Chance would be a fine thing.'

Deep down, that's exactly what she'd hoped he would say.

'So tell me, does it work? As a wooing method?' He looked at her as if challenging her to be frank and say how she felt.

So she was.

'Yes, to be honest.' She fought a flush and made herself carry on looking at him and smiling in what she hoped was a light-hearted way.

'Good,' he said, holding her gaze and echoing her smile, making her stomach flip and her throat tense up.

Then he chuckled. 'Would it be even more effective to tell you that I knit?'

'Knit? As in with wool?' She was relieved by the diversion.

'Yes, as in scarves and hats, soon to become jumpers.'

'Erm… I think that might be a bit too much information, to be honest. I'd stick with the poems.' Why did she keep saying 'to be honest'? She was spending too much time with Rick and his stock phrases.

'Okay, I'll keep the knitting to myself.'

'Good plan.' There she went again with her stock phrases.

'So tell me about you. Paula said you work at the college?'

Had he asked Paula that?

'Yes, as a CSW with the deaf students.'

'CSW is?'

'Communication support worker, a job for someone who knows some BSL but not enough to be a fully qualified interpreter.'

'Ah yes, of course, I know that. How long have you been signing?'

'Oh, six or seven years. You?'

'Well, I did level one a few years ago after I met a deaf man at this social club I go to. It's enough to help us communicate a bit better but maybe one day I'll do my level two. Why did you learn?'

'I was stuck in a job I disliked and then my partner and I split up so it just felt like a good time to start fresh.'

She didn't mention being abandoned, thrown into months of dark depression and frantic anxiety. Years of unanswered questions. Sam made her forget the hurts somehow.

'Yes, yes, I know all about new starts and adjusting to shit.'

'I'm sure you do.' She paused before saying, 'My boyfriend just walked out one day.' She wasn't really sure why she'd said that but with Sam's encouragement and gentle questioning, it all came out. How she'd come home one cold night and found Dan gone: the note, the frantic house search, telling the police, Rick's adamant theory that he'd left her for someone else, her gut feeling that that wasn't it, her needing to know where Dan was.

Sam nodded and looked at her intently, listening to her every word, and then he shook his head, 'God, Beth, that's some shit.'

'Yeah, a shitload of shit.'

Inexplicably, she felt herself smiling. Probably from having unburdened herself. Talking to Sam was a balm because he understood, he faced shit most days. It took someone who knew hardship to fully get it.

Wanting to get off this subject before she told him about her mum and Tom, her dad and the baby as well, she looked around for inspiration. 'Is that your son?' she asked, pointing at the photo.

'Yes,' his grin was back, 'Ollie. That was taken a few years ago when I was still with his mum. He's 10 now.'

'He's a beautiful boy.'

'Yes, he really is. I don't see him enough.'

'Does he come and stay here?' She glanced at the books and shoes.

'Saturdays and one weekend a month. I am trying to make him feel at home here when he comes but it's hard. Have you got kids?'

'No. No kids.' She shook her head, smiling again for some reason. They talked some more, long after they'd reached the bottom of their coffee cups, lamenting the raw deal that many loving dads get on access to their children and then just talking amicably about life. Beth's eyes were starting to prickle with tiredness. College had been as challenging as ever and it felt a long day. Sam was looking drained too.

'I'd better go, it's been a long day.'

'Sure, I think my body's telling me to lie down for a while anyway. It was great to see you, Beth, you must come again. When I'm having a good day energy-wise, I'll cook you supper.'

'I'd like that,' she said, standing up and heading for the hall. Sam followed her.

'Thanks for the coffee,' she said as she pulled on her coat and then suddenly remembered, 'Oh, how did it go with the PA?'

'I saw two in the end and liked one so I've offered the job to him. A bloke named Jack who seemed nice. He knows Sarah, funnily enough. The other was too professional and efficient for my taste. You know, detached.'

'Yeah, I know the type,' she nodded, thinking Gemma might fit in that category, too busy with protocol to be any kind of friend to a person she was supporting.

Sam opened the door. 'It's been really good to see you again,

Beth,' he repeated and he squeezed her arm as if unsure of himself for a moment.

Just the way he said her name made her feel warm.

'I agree, we'll text,' she said, liking the sound of 'we'. She headed out, her belly full of butterflies.

When she let herself in the house, all was quiet. Rick's car wasn't outside. He'd left a note on the table that read: *She's not letting me go home yet but I think she will! She says she'll need a bit of time to process this but she knows what an idiot she married and couldn't expect me not to be a prick sometimes. I'll take that! I'm going to my mate Simon's. I really owe you one for putting me up. I'll text you, R*

He'd locked the door with the spare key she'd given him and put it back through the letter box. She knew that he and Claire would work through this; they were a seasoned married couple.

The house felt quiet, yet she didn't even think about wine, just went up for a bath, feeling tired but happy.

Chapter 36

Beth had left her phone at college overnight in her haste to get to Sam's. She'd felt lost without it yesterday evening and drove to work early in order to find it before classes started. Her first stop was the treatment room, which was the last place she'd been yesterday. It wasn't there so she tried the classroom and the toilets. Nothing.

Then it occurred to her that, most likely, the cleaners had found it and taken it to lost property. Hopefully it was the cleaners and not a student who could look at her history on there in minutes. If the cleaners had found it, she had no idea where they might take it so she headed for the office.

Lee was just coming in with four takeaway coffees in a carton holder from the place round the corner. He put them down on the table as he saw her. 'Morning, Beth, got coffee, miles better than the canteen stuff. Want one?'

'No thanks, you're alright, I'm looking for my phone.' She tried to keep the anxiety from her voice. Where would the cleaners take it if they found it?

'Oh it's here, I have it. A deaf girl handed it in after you'd left. She thought it was yours but wasn't sure.'

He went round his desk and opened a drawer, pulling out her handset, and she felt herself relax, her faith in humanity momentarily restored.

'Oh God, thanks, I'm glad to see that. Maybe I will take one of those coffees after all if that's okay?'

'Sure, take one, I think I bought one too many. I forgot Gemma's off today.'

'Gemma's not in?'

'No, training day or something.'

Beth couldn't help noticing that Lee had bought a coffee for Gemma but not for her. She let that slide, not wanting to sound churlish.

177

'Do you know what she's doing?'

'Not really sure. You know Gemma, always volunteering to learn new things.'

The way Lee said it made it sound like Gemma was the goddess of acquired knowledge. Beth wondered what she'd be enthusing about knowing tomorrow. She took her coffee and excused herself, heading to the empty classroom to sit and wait for Gail in quiet isolation. Her head felt a bit groggy but, other than that, she felt no difference yet from taking the pills. The cloudy head may have nothing to do with them either and the coffee would soon sort that out.

When she switched on her phone, she found four missed calls from the same persistent 0800 number. She ignored them. There were three texts: one from her network provider offering free tickets to some upcoming sporting event, and two from Sam. She felt that flutter in her guts again. The first read:

Hi Beth, forgot to say, there is a party at the MS centre on Friday. I am asking everyone from the weekend. Starts at 7 can you come? Hope so x

It was sent just after she'd left his flat. Not stopping to reply, she opened the second, received at 9.40pm last night.

Hi Beth, did you get my text about the party Friday? Are you free?

There was no *x*. Maybe he thought she was ignoring him.

She hastily replied that she'd love to go and hoped to get a response, sipping her coffee and leafing through a book about human anatomy that someone had left out on the desk. Her phone rang, it was Sam.

'Hello?'

'Hi, Beth, are you at work?'

'I am but nobody's arrived yet so I'm not busy.'

'Cool, really glad you can come tomorrow, I was worried you hadn't got my texts.'

'Sorry, I'd left my phone at work, replied as soon as I read them. Thanks for inviting me,' she said.

'No problem, great you can come. Do you want a lift? Jack's taking the job and he's driving me there. Thought you might like to drink?'

She knew she definitely would want a drink, probably many

drinks, but she also knew that drinking was a very bad idea. Driving would give her a good reason not to give in. 'No, it's fine, thanks anyway.'

'No probs, I'll email directions.'

'Great, see you there.'

She hung up just as Gail came into the room.

'Off somewhere nice?' asked Gail, smiling.

'Party on Friday with friends I made at the weekend.'

It was a thrill to say those words. For the most part, Beth had been living these last years since Dan in a kind of self-induced isolation.

'We're doing a quiz this morning,' Gail told her. 'Basically, it's a lot of old multiple choice exam questions but don't tell them that!'

Beth was just about to ask if she could read the questions before she signed them when Gail added, 'I'll hand these out to everyone, it's all written down. I'll read them out too but Becky can just read them herself. I thought that would be easier for her and you.'

Hallelujah, Beth thought to herself. 'Yes, it definitely will, that's great.'

Was she, at last, getting somewhere toward making Gail more deaf aware?

'It means you won't have that much to do this morning apart from explaining to Becky what to do. After break, we'll go through the answers so she'll need you then. Here, take this copy of the quiz and have a look.'

Beth took the paper, feeling that she should tell Gail how impressed she was, but she didn't want to sound patronising. 'That's great, Gail, it'll really help.'

On a whim, at lunch time, Beth went along to the computer room. The morning had been full of hope but, while Becky was doing the quiz, Beth had thought of something that was still weighing on her.

She found a booth, logged on to the internet and googled the town where her dad lived in Spain. She found the nearest airport and then checked there were direct flights there from Manchester.

Just then, Lee popped his head round the door and told her there was a quick staff meeting in the office to discuss plans for the staff

Christmas party. She had finished her searches for today anyway: just looking was all she wanted to do at this stage.

Chapter 37

Sam, Friday

Sam had woken up with dead, painful legs. For a while he hadn't been able to get out of bed as he knew he'd just collapse. His wheelchair wasn't by his bed so he'd have to get himself to it. He also kept some pills for attacks like this in the drawer of his bedside cabinet. He was well prepared, like Beth said. As he reached for the pills, he first pulled out an unopened box of condoms and the irony made him smile.

By hook or by crook, he would get himself to the party. After a late breakfast, he went back to bed and slept for five more hours.

When Jack rang the doorbell at six thirty, Sam was in his best white shirt and black trousers, smelling of CK In2U and feeling ready to get out of the flat.

Jack was in his jeans, his beard recently trimmed as Sam had told him that his mouth would need to be visible for the deaf people to lip-read.

'Hi, mate. By 'eck you look gorgeous tonight, petal.' He laughed, shaking Sam's hand while Sam mimed flicking his hair and adjusting his boobs.

Sam laughed; he liked this guy. 'We've got twenty minutes or so, so you can varnish my nails for me before we go.'

Jack laughed again and Sam knew he'd made the right choice.

'Seriously, mate,' Jack asked, 'what do you need me to do before we go? Anything?'

'Well, actually, there's a bit of a pile of washing–up and I'd love it if you could put the duvet back on my bed as it fell on the floor and I've been having trouble doing much today at all.'

He went to wait in the lounge.

'All done,' said Jack, bounding into the room ten minutes later. 'Do you want me to dry the things and put them away in the kitchen?'

'Nah, that's okay, thanks, it's easier if I do it and put them where I know I'll find them.'

'Fair enough, shall we go then?'

Sam nodded and got up, hanging on to the chair arm and plonking himself back in his wheelchair.

'Lead the way, sweetheart!' Jack joked, bowing a little.

They arrived at the party earlier than Sam had thought but it was already reasonably busy in the hall. Tables were set out at one end, leaving room for a dance floor. The lights were dimmed and the DJ was playing an ABBA mix. Some youngsters, probably grandchildren, were already throwing their arms around and kicking their feet in random jerks.

There were a lot of balloons saying '40' in bright colours, and streamers and party poppers on the tables. The promised buffet was mainly thinly cut white-sliced bread sandwiches and several chocolate cakes. The bar room was open but there was also a small hatch from this side of the wall where they could order drinks. The centre had tried very hard to make the sterile room look festive.

Sam spied Gary at a table and pulled his chair up to it, making sure that he could see the door and be ready to wave the others over when they arrived. He'd barely had time to sign more than 'hi-how are you' and introduce Jack before Paula and Donna walked in, looking around for any familiar faces. Sam waved as hard as he could, and they made their way over.

They did the introductions. Sam could almost see Gary's eyes light up when Donna mentioned football. He was a huge United fan and they soon became immersed in a conversation. Paula rolled her eyes in resignation and she asked Sam if Jack signed. He told her no and then repeated the question to Jack, who shook his head and started fingerspelling A–B–C–D–E up to H, where Gary had aborted his lesson. Paula taught him the rest of the alphabet and then showed him how to sign NAME-ME-JACK by moving an 'n' hand–shape forward from his head in a two-fingered salute before pointing to himself.

While he was watching them, Izzy had arrived with her mum and was telling her how to sign her name to Paula. Someone had been to the bar and got two jugs of lager and a pile of glasses. Donna and Jack were both drinking J2O.

Sam looked at his watch; it was nearly eight already. He looked to the door and saw Danny coming in, pushed by his PA, Ellie. Before he could wave, they headed toward the food but then Beth entered behind them. She looked beautiful, with her hair tied back and wearing a purple scarf that brought colour to her face.

She caught sight of him as he waved, then came round and touched his shoulder as everyone said hello. Sam introduced her to Gary, Jack and Izzy's mum, who all shook her hand, and then asked her if she wanted a drink. Jack sprang up to get it, offering his seat to Beth.

'How's your day been?' Sam shouted over the music.

'Oh, okay, ready for the weekend. How about you?

'Slept most of it, bloody legs.' He was smiling as usual. Then he noticed Danny and Ellie coming toward them. Danny was half-twisted in his chair, trying to shout something to Ellie, who was bending down to hear him. As soon as he turned to face the front, he slammed his hands on the brakes over his wheels so that Ellie bashed into the back of him.

'Danny!' Sam yelled, 'Over here!'

But Danny had seen them before he stopped, his mouth hanging open almost as if they were in a bad, clichéd movie.

'Danny?'

He turned to try to see what Danny had seen and saw Beth with her hand clasped over her mouth, eyes wild. As he started to ask her what was going on, she got up and ran out of the room.

'Beth?!' he shouted.

'Beth, wait!' Danny echoed and spun his head round toward the door just as she disappeared.

'Danny?' Sam shouted again, 'What's going on?' And then it dawned on him. 'Oh my God, you're Dan!' Sam wheeled round the table, the others all looking on in total bemusement. 'Shit, man, you're Beth's Dan, aren't you?'

'I was, I...' he tailed off.

Jack came over. 'Everything alright, mate?'

'Have you got your keys?' Sam shouted urgently, 'We need to go after Beth!' and he started wheeling himself out, knocking into chairs and other people's legs. 'Sam, wait!' Danny shouted.

'Sam, wait!' Jack echoed, pulling up level.

Sam hoped that they'd find Beth in the car park but he had to wind his way up and down an access ramp to get out there and by the time they did, there was no sign of her or a car that looked like the one he remembered her driving.

He wheeled over to Jack's car, shouting that they had to go and find Beth. Jack didn't ask questions, just helped Sam into the car as quickly as possible, folded his chair and stored it in the boot. Sam sat in the passenger seat: he had never felt so frustrated with his body. All he wanted was to sprint to his own car and speed away.

He slammed a fist on the dashboard and then got out his phone and rang Beth. It rang several times before switching to voicemail.

'Beth, it's Sam, pick up the phone!'

Jack got in the driver's seat and started the engine, knowing how much Sam wanted to go.

'Where am I going, mate?'

'Beth's house.'

'Where's Beth's house?'

'Shit, man, wait, it's in my phone. Start driving to the ring road east.'

Jack reversed out and headed off as instructed, while Sam found the address and got a road map on his phone.

As they were driving, Jack asked what was going on.

'Sorry, Jack, I should have filled you in. Succinctly, my mate Danny, at the party, disappeared from Beth's life several years ago; they used to live together. She had no idea where he was or even if he was alive.'

'Woah. He never told Beth he was going?'

'He left her a very ambiguous note.'

Jack didn't say anything else, just focused on driving. Sam was dying to try calling Beth again but Jack needed the road map.

When they got to Beth's road, her house was dark and there was no sign of her car. Jack jumped out to look through the windows but soon came back.

'Not there.'

Sam rang again but got no answer so he texted, too, just asking her to say that she was okay. When Jack asked if he wanted to go home, Sam shook his head.

'I need to go back and talk to Danny,' he said, rubbing his temples. 'Sorry, Jack, being my PA won't normally be like this.'

Jack grinned, 'No problem, I like a bit of James Bond.' And then they headed back to the centre.

Chapter 38

When Beth got to her car, she was shaking convulsively. Her preference would have been to sit behind the wheel in the safe space it afforded her but she had to get away in case someone came looking for her.

Seeing Dan had been like seeing a ghost, and it seemed even worse as it was the first night she was out with Sam.

With no time to think about what might have happened in Dan's life to lead up to him being there, she reversed at speed and screeched out of the car park, not knowing where she was heading. The roads were pretty quiet so she drove round at random, shaking and sobbing, cursing the stars for blighting her life so much.

In a moment of clear thinking, she realised that she should go back to the centre to find out Dan's story, then turned her car in that direction. But, immediately struck by the impossible ridiculousness of the idea, she sped on past, toward her own house.

She couldn't go there, she couldn't bear it, so she stopped at the gates of a park she didn't recognise and got out of her car. It was a biting cold night, and the park was in almost pitch-darkness as she nearly lost her footing alongside the icy lake.

She sat on a bench, shivering and crying for what felt like hours, terrified of how hopeless she felt. Eventually, a group of youths drinking out of bottles and sounding aggressive, came toward her.

In a panic, she ran back to her car. 'What the fuck, Dan?!' she screamed out, punching the wheel.

The only thing she really needed now was a drink, and the idea gave her some focus. Where was a shop that would be selling? She trailed through the streets, scouring the darkened rows of shops for something that looked open, losing her bearings in a state of delirium. At last, she saw somewhere and pulled up outside.

There wasn't much choice so she took a couple of bottles of wine and, on second thoughts, a couple of bottles of whiskey, paying dis-tractedly with two £20 notes and not even waiting for the change.

She turned on the heater in her car and took a few swigs from a whiskey bottle. It almost made her gag but she swallowed it down and felt a little better; the burning sensation helped ease her gasping sobs. After a few more swigs, she realised there was only one place she could think of to go.

Chapter 39

When Sam and Jack got back to the centre, they saw Danny and Ellie sitting in the reception area. His head was in his hands.

'Is she here?' Sam almost shouted, 'Did she come back?'

Dan shook his head.

'Danny, Dan, do you have any idea where she might be? Do you have any idea what hell you put her through?'

Dan sat silently, shoulders hunched.

'Perhaps we need to hear his side, mate?' Jack put in.

Sam stopped shouting then and breathed, knowing this was true but not wanting to waste time listening. He was behaving out of character. It might help him find Beth if he slowed down.

'You're right, Jack, I'm sorry, Danny, will you explain to me?'

'I can try.'

Dan's voice was hoarse and strained. 'I feel sick, dizzy.'

Sam sent Jack for coffee and something to eat.

Dan explained as briefly as he could. 'When I was living with Beth, I'd started to get headaches and dizziness. I ignored it all for as long as possible, even the momentary losses of vision I got, until finally I had a small seizure and took myself to the doctor's.

'There were all the tests and then the diagnosis of a brain tumour. Cancer,' he went on, 'and I knew I couldn't hide it from Beth much longer. It got harder to tell her the more I learned because I hadn't told her any of it earlier on.'

'God!' was all Sam could say. He knew what that felt like.

'I wrote Beth a long letter explaining it all but ended up tearing it to shreds and leaving her a scrap. A stupid, heartless one-liner. I've tried to write to her since but wouldn't know where to start.'

Sam sat in silence, thinking. 'And now? Is the cancer gone?'

'We think so but my nerves have been damaged by the radiotherapy; now I have a condition called radio necrosis.' Dan looked at Sam. 'Can you understand?'

Sam nodded again. 'You've no idea, mate.' He could understand totally how diagnosis of illness was much more than medical. There were massive ripples affecting your emotions, your relationships, your thinking.

'Are you and Beth together?' Dan asked out of the blue, looking directly at Sam.

'I met her a week ago today,' Sam replied cagily. Dan cocked his head and tried again.

'Are you going to get together?'

Sam laughed nervously, 'Jesus, man, I just met her. I'm a crip, remember.'

'She couldn't get much better than you, Sam, and you deserve her. Look after her, won't you?'

Sam didn't answer, only nodded slightly and said, 'You have to meet her, you know. Not tomorrow but soon.'

'If she'll let me.'

'She'll let you,' Sam said, with a confidence he didn't feel. *If we find her*, he wanted to add.

'What shall we do?' he asked no one in particular.

'Do you know anywhere else she might be, Danny?' Jack asked, placing a tray of coffee and sandwiches on the floor. Dan shook his head. 'I think she'll go home. She's probably parked in a lay-by or driving round the streets, but then I think she'll go home.'

'Do you think she might come back here?'

'No,' Sam and Dan said together.

'Maybe we should call it a night, then, and look for her tomorrow?'

Sam shook his head vehemently, 'Just leave her, you mean?'

'Well, try her phone again.'

Sam called her but her phone was switched off. They'd been here too long.

'Did you see her eyes?' he asked, 'We can't just give up.' He was starting to shake. 'Do you all have any idea what she might do while we're sitting here having a tea party?'

'Well, we could go to the police?' Jack offered.

'What, and say a woman left a party an hour or so ago on a Friday

night and hasn't been seen since? They'll laugh at us.' His voice was
rising as was his panic.

Everyone looked at him, at a loss.

'She could do anything!' he repeated.

'Then we'll get back in the car and keep looking.'

'Let's go!'

'You've barely touched your coffee.'

'Forget the damned coffee!'

Once they were back in the car, Jack headed on a circuitous route
back to Beth's house. He didn't know what her car was like and Sam
barely did either. 'Small and silver, I think,' was all Sam could manage, and so it was a fairly pointless drive, especially as Sam was busy
replying to a worried text from Gary and not even looking out of
the window.

Jack soon turned into Beth's road but her house was still dark.
He pulled up and told Sam that he'd go and have another look. As
Jack was ringing the doorbell and peering through any windows he
could get to, Sam pulled out his phone, tried Beth's number and got
nothing, so texted her again:

Beth, it's Sam, where are you? We're worried! He pressed send and
then, as an afterthought, texted again: *I talked to Danny*, he erased the
final 'ny', *I talked to Dan, you'll understand his story. The idiot thought
leaving would protect you. Talk to me xx*

Jack got in the car and looked at Sam. 'Almost sure she's not there.
Even if she's hiding, there's no car.'

Sam sighed wearily.

'We should go home, Sam, get some sleep and she'll turn up
tomorrow.'

'Sleep?!' But he knew Jack was right. 'Alright, let's go home.'

It wasn't alright to Sam, he couldn't bear not knowing if she'd
done something stupid. He was too tired to argue, though, and he
saw that there was nothing they could do now.

There was a small, silver car parked on the road in front of Sam's
place when they drove up. Jack pulled up and looked questioningly

at Sam. 'It looks like the one I remember,' he said, pulling off his seat belt.

They got out as fast as they could, what with the wheelchair to manage, and Jack helped push an exhausted Sam up the gravel drive. There was a dark figure sitting on the door ramp, drinking something straight from a bottle. They hurried up to her.

'Beth?'

'Sam?' she said, although there was enough light to see him clearly. He couldn't help smiling. He reached forward and took the bottle from her hands. It still felt fairly full, so she can't have been here very long, unless this was her second bottle. There were no empties. He handed the bottle to Jack, along with his door key, and watched as he let himself in and put the whiskey on the table.

'I'll be off then.' Jack said. 'I guess you guys need to talk. Glad to see you, Beth,' and with that, he jogged back to his car.

'How long have you been here?' Sam asked, not able to see Beth's face.

'Not that long.' He heard more of a slur in her voice this time.

'We were very worried.'

'I'm sorry,' she whimpered, and collapsed into a ball. 'All I ever do is fuck up. My life is just one big fuck–up.'

Sam didn't know what to do; he needed Jack. He couldn't possibly pull her up. 'Let's go inside,' he coaxed, hopefully, 'it's bloody freezing out here and I'm dog–tired.' Beth didn't move.

'Beth? Come on, I'm a crip in a chair, you've got to help me out here.' She looked up then so he went on, 'Come on, Beth, get up and help me inside, please.' She seemed to respond and tried to get herself up. 'Bit pished,' she managed, staggering to her feet.

'Hold my chair, it'll keep you balanced, and give me a push up the ramp.'

She did as she was told but not too effectively: Sam was glad he had a self-propelling wheelchair but it took all the strength he could muster to wheel himself inside. Beth collapsed on the sofa while he went to make strong, sugary tea.

'Bit of a sugar fix,' he said, wheeling back in, trying to lighten things. Sam looked at her; she'd taken her hair down. Her eyes were still roaming but he found her face beautiful. She sat on the other end of the sofa, not speaking, knees pulled up to her chest.

After a few minutes of silent tea-drinking, Sam said, 'I talked to Danny.' She flinched slightly but said nothing. 'He told me his story, Beth. You'll have to hear it from him one day but he told me pretty much all of it.' He paused and she looked at him, still silent but giving him permission to go on. He told her the story of Dan being diagnosed with brain cancer, not daring to tell her, caring too much to see straight.

She breathed steadily and he could see the rise and fall of her diaphragm until eventually she said: 'So he thought not telling me would hurt less than sharing his illness with me?'

'Well, yes,' Sam's voice was gentle, 'that's what he said. He knows now how irrational that was. You'll have to talk to him, Beth, you can ask him, he'll talk to you. He wants to talk to you.'

He saw Beth flinch again.

'Maybe not tomorrow but soon, when you're ready.'

She breathed some more and he reached over to squeeze her hand and she squeezed back.

'You'll know when and what's best. You're strong.'

Beth slid toward him on the sofa and put her head on his chest. His arm went round her shoulders. They sat in exhausted silence until Sam's arm cramped and they both needed the toilet. Then they went to his bed and spooned as they fell asleep, not even needing to speak.

Chapter 40

Beth hovered outside the door to the café, wishing Sam had been well enough to see her this morning for a pep talk. It had taken her months to get the courage to fix up a meeting and ever since she had, she'd been dreading it.

Taking a deep breath, she went in and spotted him at a table in the corner. He had started growing a beard and had gained some weight but was still recognisably the same person. She had expected there to be a PA with him, but he was alone.

Swallowing, she walked over to him and sat opposite.

'Hello, Dan.'

'Hello, Beth.'

They looked at each other. Where could they possibly start?

'This is a nice café, do you come here a lot?' Beth found herself saying, cringing inside at the platitude.

To his credit, Dan managed to answer without showing any signs of noticing it.

A waitress came over then and they ordered coffee.

'So,' Dan said without further preamble, 'it was a great shock to see you at the MS centre.'

His voice sounded different, slightly slurred by his illness.

'I guessed it was inevitable we'd run into each other one day,' he continued soberly, 'but I never expected it to be there. I'm quite surprised it didn't happen sooner, but then I don't do much to get me out any more.'

Beth was glad that at least Dan was going to talk but she didn't know what he expected her to say and waited for him to go on.

'I owe you an explanation, a very big explanation.'

Beth nodded.

'I'm sure Sam has shared what I told him?'

'Yes, I still find it very hard to understand why you felt you couldn't tell me.' She heard a catch in her voice and swallowed.

195

'I meant to so many times, Beth, do know that. Like I think I said to Sam, the longer I left it, the harder it got. I didn't want to bring any more trauma to your life, I guess.'

'And so you thought it better to just disappear and leave me wondering if you were dead?' Her voice was rising.

'No,' he paused for a second and checked himself. 'Yes, I suppose I did. I tried to write many times but I couldn't find the words.'

The coffee arrived then before she got a chance to explode at him. She tried to breathe, missing Sam.

'I'm so sorry, Beth, I can't explain more than I have.'

'When you'd first left,' Beth said, trying to keep her voice level, 'everyone kept telling me you must have another woman, that I should hate you. I did hate you a lot of the time,' Dan looked down at his lap in shame, 'but I also told myself that one day you'd come back with a perfectly simple and forgivable explanation and we'd live happily ever after.'

'Beth, I'm sorry,' he shook his head as if in disbelief at how it had turned out.

'I'll never understand why you didn't tell me but now that you have, I can't hate you or love you. I know you must have been going through torment, so one day I will forgive you, but I can't forget the torment you inflicted on me.'

'I understand.'

Beth felt like she was talking to someone other than Dan. He hadn't just changed physically – their lives had drifted so far apart emotionally too. She didn't know if she wanted to see him any more.

They both fell quiet. Beth felt that they both knew there was nothing else to say.

'Look, Dan, like I say, I don't hate you any more. I'm glad I know you're okay and I'm glad I saw you. If I see you again at the MS centre or anywhere else, I will say hello but I'm not going to say we should stay friends because I know we won't.'

'Right, yes.' He nodded and repeated, 'Yes, you're right.'

Beth stood up to leave, her coffee untouched. She couldn't stay any longer, reminded of the hell she'd been through years before.

'I've got to go,' she blurted without further explanation.

'Yes, okay.' He seemed stuck for words too. 'Well, see you, Beth.'

'Yeah, I guess you will.' She walked out as quickly as she could, aware of a familiar buzzing sound building in her head.

Driving home, she felt hugely destabilised from seeing him. She really didn't want to see him again because it was just going to stir up so much angst. She was relieved to know where Dan was but now that she knew, her hurt seemed somehow exacerbated by feeling angry at him and then feeling guilty for feeling angry. She wanted to see Sam but he still needed his rest.

She hadn't felt like this for months. She was off the pills as she'd disliked the feeling of being in a numbed limbo, unable to feel low but unable to feel much joy either. The course of CBT she was on now had been helping so much but seeing Dan had made every-thing she'd learned go out of her head.

She'd been stupid to schedule this when Sam was still ill. They were like ships passing in the night at the moment. Ever since he'd come out of hospital, once the worst of the infection was over, they hadn't found a time for her to visit him. Either she was at work or doing her BSL course, or he was asleep or too weak for com-pany. Suddenly the awful suspicion arose that she had misjudged how strongly they felt toward each other.

She wondered what to do with herself, feeling jumpy and strangely wired. Her laptop was on the sofa so she opened it idly. There were about five emails from *nostrings*, counting down to the deadline, after six months, when her profile would be permanently deleted, and enticing her to reactivate it for free in just one click. It felt like old times: she hadn't heard from or thought of *nostrings* since meeting Sam. In a daze, she clicked on the link and within ten min-utes got a message from *Jason3* asking her where she'd been and if she wanted to *have some fun*.

Yes, she typed.

While he was on his way, she panicked and had second thoughts. What in hell was she doing? This wasn't what you did when you had fallen in love with someone like Sam. Self-loathing kicked in.

Jason3 rang the bell and, as soon as she opened the door, he announced beaming, 'I have a rucksack full of toys for us.' He looked barely legal age.

Beth just stared at him, feeling sick. 'I made a mistake, Jason, is that your name? I don't want you to be here.'

Before he could answer, she shut the door in his face and crumpled down on to the ground behind it.

She had no idea how long she sat there before her phone rang. It was Rick.

'Hello.'

'Just ringing to see how Sam is, and how you are.'

'I still haven't seen Sam since he came out of hospital. We do speak on the phone occasionally but we don't even seem able to choreograph calls at the moment. I get home from work, he's ready to sleep. Weekends are mostly taken up with my level 6 BSL. When I get him, he sounds okay, definitely recovering.'

'That's good to hear. And you? How are you, Beth?'

'I'm having a terrible day.' She felt a sob welling up at the relief of unloading.

'What's up?'

'I had an awful meeting with Dan this morning, it's taken so long to arrange but I still had no clue what to say. Just texting Sam isn't much working for me either, I'm worried it's all going to crumble with him.' She felt she was garbling and left out the *Jason3* episode. Tears were running down her cheeks.

'You met Dan?! Don't let him worry you after what he did to you.'

'But I do, I feel I can't be angry with him now I know his story.'

'But you are angry?'

Beth rubbed her eyes. 'I don't know what to think.'

'Well, don't think then, it's overrated anyway.'

She gave a little laugh; good old Rick.

'You can feel angry if you feel angry,' he said, 'I would feel bloody angry.'

'You're a good friend, Rick, thank you.'

'Don't get all soft, Beth, that Sam's turning you into some kind of Da–lay Lama.'

'It's pronounced Dalai and hardly!' she was feeling better.

'Whatever. And as for Sam, he is poorly, not ignoring you on purpose, you must know that? He loves you, idiot.'

She *was* an idiot for ever having had doubts. 'Talking of lurve, how's Claire?'

'Claire is the same as ever, you know, she keeps me in line.'

Beth remembered a phone call with Claire, not long after Claire had thrown Rick out. She had taken him back but only after making sure he knew she knew he was an idiot.

'I married a prick,' she told Beth on the phone. 'I knew that I was marrying a prick and I still chose to marry him. I can hardly expect him never to be a prick, now can I?'

Beth was incredulous that Claire barely mentioned her having played any part in events, and their friendship seemed undamaged. Rick seemed just the same as ever, cracking jokes and being a prick.

'How's work?' he was asking now.

'It's okay, better than before, they're learning. Paula came in to do a deaf awareness session for all the staff. And the girl I don't like, Gemma, is leaving to work in a school with younger kids. Since I'm doing my level 6, I'll hopefully make it as an interpreter, then I can leave too.'

'While I'm stuck forever with crock-of-shit.'

'That's not forever, remember your B&B idea.'

'Yeah yeah, blah blah.'

'Look, we're down at your level of childishness, I should go. I need to try Sam before it's too late for him.'

After the call, Beth felt a lot better. It had made her remember the good stuff that was happening at the moment. This had been a really trying day but, she realised, she'd got through it pretty unscathed.

Chapter 41

It was another week before Beth finally saw Sam again. She took him out for a late lunch at a pub overlooking a nearby reservoir. It was a sunny, warm day so they sat outside on the terrace.

He got hold of her hand over the table, looking drawn and embattled.

'I really missed you, Beth.'

'I know, I did too.' She felt a twinge of guilt but suppressed it.

'Tell me more about your meeting with Danny? You hardly said anything on the phone. I haven't even seen him at the MS centre since the party.'

'It was just weird, he's changed so much. Not just how he is physically, he just feels so different to the Dan I remember.'

'It's possible the tumour's changed his personality.'

'I guess, or I have been holding a false image of him.'

'Possible too.'

'I still just can't understand him disappearing like that.'

'Maybe you never will. You can't analyse it forever.'

'I know, Rick said the same. He said thinking is overrated.'

'Well, not sure about that. I'm more of an "I think therefore I am" kind of guy.'

'I know *that's* true!'

'And if *you* stopped thinking, we'd have to change your name-sign again.'

Beth laughed.

'I *think*,' he emphasised the word, 'that at times of big trauma, we all do irrational things.'

'I guess.'

'Do you ever think about the night you saw him at the MS centre?'

'Do I think about it? Of course I do!'

'I mean,' he squeezed her hand, 'when you ran out. Your phone was off, I searched and searched knowing how upset you'd be. I was really worried you might harm yourself or crash your car.'

'I am really sorry.'

'No, it's not that. I don't want you to feel bad. I just mean that you did a mini Dan disappearance on me. No one can think straight once adrenaline and hormones start messing with your head.'

'You're right as usual.' She sighed. 'You're so wise. Maybe that should be your new name-sign.'

'Maybe it should, I don't feel like a fireman any more, but if I am Sam-wise, would that make you Frodo?'

Beth laughed again, 'God, you do me good.'

'Good, I try my best.' He smiled as he said, 'On that note, I must say that I did something very rash this morning.'

'I did something very rash last night.' Beth chimed in.

Just then, the waiter came over with their bowls of spinach and mushroom risotto served with salmon steak.

'Wow, that looks good,' Beth said.

'Totally nutritious.'

'That's all you ever think about.'

'Pfft. Anyway, like I was saying, I did a very rash thing this morning and I want to tell you my rash thing first.'

'Go on then.'

'Well, whether or not it will go ahead kind of depends on your answer to this question.'

'Right.'

He took a breath to prepare himself and reached out for her hand again: 'Will you live with me, Beth?'

She didn't hesitate in declaring 'Yes!' but then Sam saw her face drop.

'Is it too soon?'

'It's soon, Sam, but it doesn't feel at all too soon. Just thinking, where? Your flat's too small and…'

'Ah but that's where my rash thing comes in,' he interrupted. 'When I was out with Jack earlier, we saw the details of a bungalow in an estate agent's window. I went in to ask about it and the girl there said we could go straight to see it.'

'Great.'

'Well, looking round, I loved it and could really see us there. You know, you and me.'

'That's a lovely thought.'

'So I made an offer on it, which has been accepted.'

Beth was stunned to silence.

'Obviously I can pull out if you don't like it.'

'Sam, that's amazing!'

'Thank God!'

She went round to kiss him, not caring that people were looking.

'It's a new start, Sam.' She went back to her seat. 'Can we call it Becher's bungalow?'

'I love it! There is plenty of space so we can have Becher's themed parties too.'

Beth held up her glass.

'To us,' they clinked.

'To life!' Sam said and they clinked again.

'Promise me one thing, though,' he said, sobering in tone.

'What's that?'

'Promise me that we're not expecting happily ever after. We both know life will throw God knows what at us.'

'I promise. We're ready for anything though, don't you think?'

'I hope so, Beth.'

They sat in silence for a bit, breathing in the view.

'So what's your rash thing?' Sam broke in.

'It is,' she paused and did a drum roll on the table, 'I booked us a holiday.'

'You did?!'

'We're going to the south of Spain next month. I found a hotel that sounds very accessible and it's right on the beach.'

'Beth! Fantastic! Thank you.'

'There *is* something else I need to do out there.'

He looked quizzical and then the penny dropped. 'You're going to see your dad!'

'And meet my sister. They don't know yet so I can still chicken out.'

She sat back and looked out at the water, feeling nervous already.

'Wow, too much to take in, isn't it?'

'Yes it is.'

'You are an incredibly amazing person, Beth.'

She felt suddenly guilty: she knew that she wasn't that person.

'I need to tell you something, Sam.'

'Uh–oh.'

'After I saw Dan, my head was all fucked and I rejoined *nostrings*.'

Sam closed his eyes as she continued. 'Someone came to the house but when he arrived, I sent him away again.'

Sam was silent and she worried that he would be angry that she had even thought of sleeping with another man.

Instead, he broke into a huge smile. 'Beth, you scared me there. All I can say is thank you.'

'I wasn't expecting a thank you.'

'Well, it's a thank you for telling me and a thank you for resisting. That's what we need from now on, no secrets.'

'No secrets.'

'Come here and sit on my lap.'

She walked round to his side of the table and he wrapped her in his arms.

'Listen to my wisdom,' he said in a fake Russian accent, 'we all make mistakes in life and we all mess up but when we do we must not hide it or beat ourselves up about it, understand?' She nodded.

'Now listen carefully, I will say this only once, it is a very profound observation that no one has ever made before. Are you ready, Beth?' More nodding. 'Just remember this and you'll be fine. However much you think you have messed up, you have an excuse.'

'Just get to the point.'

'We all mess up Beth, because,' he put his hands on her shoulders and punctuated his words with tiny slaps, 'We. Are. Only. Human.'

Acknowledgements

Not sure where to start so I'll try to work chronologically.

I owe a huge thanks to all the human beings I have been lucky enough to meet and who have inspired the characters in *Senseless*.

I am grateful to initial readers of my earliest complete manuscripts who gave me some useful pointers and were sufficiently enthusiastic to encourage me to send it to agents and publishers. My big five readers were: Debbie Watkins, Laura Sheard, Katherine Baldwin, Andrew Wight and Jill Lickley. I hope you love the final result!

Unreserved thanks to all the incredible team at Unbound for seeing potential in this novel and accepting to publish it. And I must mention Jen Rhodes, who did a fantastic job at filming the pitch video, adding excellent voice-over and subtitles.

Unrivalled thanks to all of you who pledged to support *Senseless* during the Crowdfunding stage. We hit the target incredibly quickly due to many enormously generous pledges.

Finally, my greatest thanks go to my editors, Gill Harvey, Holly Miller and Susanne Hillen, without whose careful and insightful direction *Senseless* would not be the book you have just read.

If you have enjoyed reading it, please review it on Goodreads, Amazon or any other platform and encourage other people to read it too. Honest reviews can make so much difference to the success of a novel in today's over-crowded market.

Thank you for reading.

Patrons

Imogen Addy
Lisa Baldock
Lilian Baldwin
Christina Bambury
Paul Barnes
Gemma Boardman
Jean Booth
Patricia Braithwaite
Cheryl Buley
Patricia Busfield
Caroline Butcher
Barbara Chuter
Gilly Cobbin
Jessica Cook
Jackie Davie
Peta Dean
Natalya Dell
Sandra Duff
Sam Egerton – Kemp
Barbara Falloon
Catherine Farmbrough
Emma Farnden
Melanie Fenemore
Sarah Finnigan
Ann Fisher
Ghislaine Fletcher
Katy Foot
Juliet Grant
Penny Gunn
Hilary Harland
Mike Harrington
Judith Hillary

Jill Hipson
Margaret Hird
Gloria Jennings
Esther Jradeh
Lynn Lawson
Janet Leach
Henrietta Longden
Jane Lowe
Camilla Maclaverty
Elizabeth Mardell (Milly)
Janet McGarry
Sarah McGeehan
Suzi McGowan
Martin McLean
Carol Moles
Laura Morris-Vangrove
Kim Olivier
David Pentland
Melissa Peters
Rosamund Pickford
Carolyn Simes
Miranda Smith
Sarah Spencer
Joanna Stevens
John Swainston
YL Tan
Iain Thake
Sam Todd
Andrew Tween
Rachel Walker
Phil Watson
Roger Webb
Megan Welford
Mary Wells
Cecelia White
Julia Wood